THE
GREAT
GODDEN

THE
GREAT
GODDEN

MEG ROSOFF

CANDLEWICK PRESS

Copyright © 2020 by Meg Rosoff

First US edition 2021
First published by Bloomsbury (UK) 2020

Library of Congress Catalog Card Number pending
ISBN 978-1-5362-1585-4

21 22 23 24 25 26 LBM 10 9 8 7 6 5 4 3 2 1

Printed in Melrose Park, IL, USA

This book was typeset in Adobe Garamond Pro.

Candlewick Press
99 Dover Street
Somerville, Massachusetts 02144

www.candlewick.com

For Catherine and Michael

And we are put on earth a little space,
That we may learn to bear the beams of love.

William Blake

1

Everyone talks about falling in love like it's the most miraculous, life-changing thing in the world. Something happens, they say, and you know. You look into the eyes of your beloved and see not only the person you've always dreamed you'd meet, but the *you* you've always secretly believed in, the you that inspires longing and delight, the you no one else really noticed before.

That's what happened when I met Kit Godden.

I looked into his eyes and I knew.

Only, everyone else knew too. Everyone else felt exactly the same way.

2

Every year when school ends we jam the car full of indispensable junk and head to the beach. By the time six people have crammed their bare essentials into the car, Dad says he can't see out the windows and there's no room for any of us, so half of everything is removed but it doesn't seem to help; I always end up sitting on a tennis racket or a bag of shoes. By the time we set off, everyone's in a foul mood.

The drive is a nightmare of shoving and arguing and Mum shouting that if we don't all pipe down she's going to have a breakdown and once a year Dad actually pulls over to the side of the road and says he'll just sit there till everyone shuts the fuck up.

We've been coming to the beach since we were born, and on the theory that life existed even before that, Dad's been coming since he was a child, and Mum since she met Dad and gave birth to us four.

The drive takes hours but eventually we come off the motorway and that's when the mood changes. The familiarity of the route does something to our brains and we start to whine silently, like dogs approaching a park. It's half an hour precisely from the roundabout to the house and we know every inch of landscape on the way. Bonus points are earned for deer or horses glimpsed from car windows or an owl sitting on a fence post or Harry the Hare hopping down the road. Harry frequently appears in the middle of the road on the day we arrive and then again on the day we leave — incontrovertible proof that our world is a sophisticated computer simulation.

There's no such thing as a casual arrival. We pull into the grass drive, scramble out of the car, and then shout and shove our way into the house, which smells of ancient upholstery, salt, and musty stale air till we open all the windows and let the sea breeze pour through in waves.

The first conversation always goes the same way:

MUM (*dreamy*): I miss this place so much.
KIDS: So do we!
DAD: If only it were a little closer.
KIDS: And had heat.
MUM (*stern voice*): Well, it's not. And it doesn't.
So stop dreaming.

No one bothers to mention that she's the one who brings the subject up every time.

Mum's already got out the dustpan and is sweeping dead flies off the windowsills while Dad puts food away and makes tea. I run upstairs, open the drawer under my bed, and pull on last summer's faded sweatshirt. It smells of old house and beach and now so do I.

Alex is checking bat-box cameras on his laptop and Tamsin's unpacking at superhuman speed because Mum says she can't go down to see her horse until everything's put away. The horse doesn't belong to her but she leases him for the summer and would save him in a fire hours before she'd save any of us.

Mattie, who's recently gone from too-big features and no tits to looking like a sixteen-year-old sex goddess, has changed into sundress and wellies and is drifting around on the beach because she sees her life as one long Instagram post. At the moment, she imagines she looks romantic and gorgeous, which unfortunately she does.

There's a sudden excited clamor as Malcolm and Hope arrive downstairs to welcome us to the beach. Gomez, Mal's very large, very mournful basset hound, bays at the top of his lungs. Tamsin and Alex will be kissing him all over, so really you can't blame him.

Mal clutches two bottles of cold white wine and while everyone is hugging and kissing, Dad mutters, "It's about time," abandons the tea, and goes to find a corkscrew. Tam hurls herself at Mal, who sweeps her up in his arms and swings her around like she's still a little girl.

Hope makes us stand in order of age: me, Mattie, Tamsin, and Alex. She steps back to admire us all, saying how much we've grown and how gorgeous we all are, though it's obvious she's mainly talking about Mattie. I'm used to being included in the gorgeous-Mattie narrative, which people do out of politeness. Tam snorts and breaks rank, followed by Alex. It's not like we don't see them in London, but between school and work, and what with living in completely different parts of town, it happens less than you might think.

"There's supper when you're ready," Hope calls after them.

Dad wipes the wineglasses with a tea towel, fills them, and distributes the first glass of the summer to the over-eighteens, with reduced rations for Mattie, Tamsin, and me. Alex reappears and strikes like a rat snake when Hope leaves her glass to help Mum with a suitcase. He downs it in two gulps and slithers away into the underbrush. Hope peers at the empty glass with a frown but Dad just fills it again.

Everyone smiles and laughs and radiates optimism. This year is going to be the best ever — the best weather, the best food, the best fun.

The actors assembled, the summer begins.

3

Our house is picturesque and annoying in equal measure. For one thing it's smaller than it looks, which is funny because most houses are the opposite. My great-great-grandfather built it for his wife as a wedding present in 1913, constructed in what Mum calls Post-Victorian-Mad-Wife-in-the-Attic style. It stayed in the family till the 1930s, when my ancestor had to sell it to pay off gambling debts. His son (my great-grandfather) bought it back twenty years later, restored the original periwinkle blue, and thereafter everyone refrained from mentioning the time it left the family. He also built a house down the beach for family overflow, which is now owned by Hope. Since Mal came on the scene, we think of it as their house, even though technically it's not.

Our house was built as a summer place, a kind of folly, not to be lived in year-round, so we don't. It's drafty, has no insulation, and the pipes freeze if you don't drain them and fill the toilets with antifreeze in November, but we love every tower and turret and odd-shaped window and even the short staircase that ends in a cupboard. My great-great-grandfather must have had a great-great sense of humor because everything in the house is pointlessly idiosyncratic. But you can see the sea from nearly every window.

My bedroom is the watchtower. Most people wouldn't want it because it's ridiculously small, no room to swing a rat. Someone tall enough could touch all four walls at once by lying flat with arms and legs outstretched. The tower comes with a built-in captain's bed and a ladder, and the ladder goes up to a tiny widow's walk, so named because women needed a place to walk while gazing out to sea through the telescope, waiting for their husbands to come back. Or not. Hence widow.

I am the possessor of the brass telescope that belonged to my great-grandfather. He was in the navy and in his later years spent a lot of time doing what

I do—standing in the square tower with his telescope trained outward. I have no idea what he saw—probably the same things I do: boats, Jupiter, owls, hares, foxes, and the occasional naked swimmer. It's kind of an unwritten rule that the telescope goes with the room. No one takes a vote; it just gets handed to the right person. Theoretically, the telescope and the room might have gone to Mattie, Tamsin, or Alex, but it didn't.

There are lots of traditions in my family, like the passing down of this house and the passing down of the telescope. On the other hand, we're distinctly lacking in the kind of traditions grand families have, like naming every oldest son Alfred or being feebleminded, and there's no sign of the gambling gene reemerging, so that's kind of a relief. But, wobble aside, when it comes to keeping property in the family from one generation to the next we're practically on a par with the Queen.

On the other side of the house is a turret. Before we four were born, Mum and Dad used the turret as a bedroom, which was romantic but impractical as it threatens to blow away from the house altogether in a high wind. About five years ago they moved down a floor to a room-shaped room over the kitchen. Mum makes costumes for the National Opera, so the turret became her summer workroom. Alex's room is across the hall and everyone calls it the cutthroat. I used to think that was because of some murky historical murder, but Dad says it's because it's so small it makes you want to cut your throat. On the plus side, it has a hexagonal window and feels snug as the berth of a boat.

Mattie and Tamsin shared a room for ages, but once Mattie hit twelve they had to be separated to prevent bloodshed. Even Mum and Dad realized that no one on earth could live with Mattie, so she ended up sole proprietor of the little guest house in the garden, which makes her feel exactly as special as she imagines she is. Tamsin has the room all to herself now, which suits everyone, as it smells powerfully of horse.

Between the bedrooms is a long landing with a built-in window seat where you can stretch out and read or meet to play cards or look out the big window to the sea. The cotton cover on the window seat is so faded it's hard to tell what color it once was. When we were little we used to call this area the playroom, but it's actually just a corridor.

Outside, the house is decorated with Victorian curlicue gables and brackets, so even the fishermen stop to take pictures on their phones. It doesn't help that it's painted periwinkle blue. When I asked Dad why we couldn't paint it a slightly less conspicuous color, he shrugged and said, "It's always been periwinkle blue," which is the sort of thing you get a lot in my family. Mindless eccentricity.

Hope is Dad's much younger cousin; Dad was twenty-two when Hope was born. Since they got together, Mal and Hope started staying at the little house every summer. It's only a hundred meters down the beach from ours and it's built of wood and glass, very modern for its time, with big wooden decks where everyone can sit and eat and look out at the sea.

Malcolm met Hope at drama school. No one thought the relationship would last because she seemed far too sensible to settle down with an actor. But they've been together for twelve years and we refer to them as Malanhope like they're a single entity. Where's Malanhope? Are Malanhope coming for dinner?

"I hope Malcolm doesn't lose Hope," Dad says at least once a week, though in fact the joke is particularly stupid given how devoted Hope is to Malcolm. We are too—he's insanely handsome and an indefatigable player of board games.

Mal and Hope are both in their early thirties and far more interesting than our parents. They're ringleaders in all things summery—drunkenness, indiscreet conversations, all-night poker. They both started out as actors, but Hope decided one day that she hated auditions and hated being poor, so now she teaches drama at a university in Essex. Occasionally she does voice-overs because she's a brilliant mimic, unlike Mal. All Mal's accents sound Irish and his attempts to speak with an American accent are pitiful. None of us has ever said it out loud, but it should probably be Hope earning a living as an actor and Mal teaching drama.

I saw Hope onstage once, playing Nora in *A Doll's House*. I was only thirteen but you had to be blind not to see how good she was. I'd never seen anyone do so little and express so much, and I never forgot it. When Malcolm acts, he throws his whole heart and soul around the stage like a rubber chicken.

We adore Mal. He teaches us stuff like sword fighting and how to laugh convincingly onstage. Mattie flirts with him, but she flirts with all forms of human life, so it's barely notable. Malcolm flirts back so as not to hurt her feelings. Mattie isn't stupid, but sometimes I think she's the most trivial person I know. She says she wants to be a doctor but her brain seems mostly filled with sex and shoes.

Mattie's just wandered back up from the water. No one there to admire her but the fish. She shouts to no one in particular that she's going down the beach to help Hope with supper.

I can hear Tamsin arguing with Dad about giving her a ride to the barn. There's a sort of policy that Tam is allowed to have Duke for the summer but doesn't get a lift up every time she has a whim to go and see him. She's right that it takes five minutes to drive and twenty to cycle, but if you add up all the five minutes she'll require in the course of a summer, Dad's right to nip it in the bud.

Mum ends the discussion and for a few blissful moments there's peace.

4

"I have two surprises," Hope said the morning after we arrived, but she wouldn't tell us either of them right away no matter how much everyone begged. "I'll tell you at supper."

I don't like surprises. Just the facts, ma'am — delivered without the champagne and sneaky smiles.

It was nearly six when I broke off from the book I was reading and looked out the window. Tam, in jodhpurs, walked back along the beach toward ours, holding a large plate of what looked like seaweed but probably had something to do with supper.

With my telescope I can see a good deal of the beach

and everything between the house and the sea. I don't look into people's bedrooms, but what happens outdoors is fair game. I can see the horizon well enough to read the names on cargo ships. I can see people in the sea well enough to lip-read conversations, if only I could read lips. At the moment, we're a couple of days off a full moon and I like its watery shades of blue, like the ghost of a real moon.

There's a general buzz around the house concerning Hope's two surprises. I wonder if she's going to announce that she's pregnant, and if so, whether this is entirely good news. Much as I love Mal, he's the sort of person who would think nothing of exchanging a baby for a handful of magic beans. Though if he did, he'd manage to convince everyone he'd done the right thing and only Hope would be cross. Mal's most useful quality is a wretched excess of charm that makes everyone ignore his flaws. But he's good to talk to when you're fed up with life or can't stand your family, because he listens, which hardly anyone else seems to do.

I can see the parents heading off for a swim, which they often do at this hour. Mum's in a green-and-white-striped swimsuit and the Panama hat Dad bought for her birthday last year. Dad's in shorts and flip-flops. They walk close together.

After the swim, Mum will light the barbecue and Dad will marinate and fuss. Malanhope will drift over with more plates of salads and bottles of wine, which will be opened. And drunk. Adults will be drunk. Children might be drunk too if no one's paying attention.

What I can't see from my window I can imagine with perfect clarity. Right now, for instance, on the floor of their living room Mal is playing chess with Alex. Mal is wincing every time Alex makes a decent move. They both cheat like pirates and no one else will play with them. I can't remember if Alex always cheated or if it's something he's picked up from Mal, who claims to be studying the criminal mind in case he ever gets cast as Moriarty.

Eventually I drift downstairs. Hope arrives and everyone wants to know what the secrets are but she insists it isn't yet time. Mal says he'll take bribes but only in cash.

"Oh for Christ's sake," mutters Alex. "This had better be good."

Mattie is starry-eyed and assumes, the way she assumes everything, that the secrets will involve her. In this, she is not entirely wrong.

It is half past eight by the time we all sit down to eat. The table is lit by proper hurricane lamps, with candle stubs in jars for backup. Alex has positioned himself at the bottom of the table so when Mal holds out the bottle to top everyone up, Mum and Dad won't notice that one of the glasses is his.

At last Hope stands up and taps the side of her glass with a spoon, like everyone isn't totally on the edge of their seats waiting for this moment anyway. A great cheer erupts from the Alex end of the table and there's a thump as Tamsin elbows him off the end of the bench onto the ground. He stays there, giggling.

"I promised two surprises," Hope says. Rather pompously, I think. She's nervous.

"Twins?" pipes up Dad, and Mal chokes.

"Not twins," Hope says. "But Mal and I are getting married. So you never know."

Mal mutters, "God forbid," but everyone else is cheering and leaning over the table to congratulate them. Hope pushes them off.

"Oh, please," she says. "We've been living together long enough."

Dad reaches across to shake Mal's hand. "Well done, Mal."

Hope rolls her eyes. "For finding a woman and chasing her to ground?"

Dad laughs.

"The wedding is the last weekend of the summer, nothing fancy, just a short service. No relatives other than immediate, a few close friends, nice meal, no party tent. Simple simple simple."

"Like Mal."

Mum shushes Alex.

"No white dress?" Mattie looks distraught.

"Mal can wear whatever he likes," answers Hope. And at last they kiss, a sweet comedy kiss.

We cheer.

Hope holds up one hand. "One last thing. Given that pretty much all the family I have left in the world is sitting here tonight, I'd like to take this moment to thank you for being nicer and less maddening than you might be. That is all."

In an example of his lifelong ability to steal a scene, Alex throws up in the long grass. Mum grabs him by the collar and drags him indoors. We hear muffled shouting, and when he finally emerges we can see that he's greenish. Mum follows with a bucket of water, looking cross.

"Can I be maid of honor?" Mattie has already chosen her dress and the flowers she'll carry.

"What about me?" says Tamsin.

"Two flower girls . . ." Hope says. "Unless you . . . or Alex?" Hope peers at me, anxious all of a sudden.

"No, thank you," I say. "Unless you particularly want us."

Hope smiles and shakes her head. "Two is plenty."

Alex perks up. "What about me?" His eyes point in completely different directions.

"What about you, my darling? I'd love to have you as a flower girl."

Alex is overjoyed. He lurches sideways.

"Enough about the wedding," says Dad. "What's the second surprise?"

The rest of us have forgotten the second surprise. "Ah," says Mal. "Well. Not all of you will be aware that Hope's godmother is Florence Godden."

"Not *the* Florence Godden?" Dad and Mal are like a worn-out old vaudeville act. Being Florence Godden's goddaughter is one of the most significant facts about Hope.

Alex lists sideways again.

"Florence is shooting a film in Hungary and the date has been moved up on short notice. So her boys are coming from LA to stay with us for the summer."

"Oh my God." Mattie looks as if she's going to

19

faint. "I can't believe you didn't tell us."

"She's telling us now, Mattie." Even Tamsin talks down to Mattie.

"I haven't seen them for years," Hope says. "I suspect they've changed. Kit must be nineteen or thereabouts and Hugo a year or two younger. You kids aren't to swamp them all at once. Remember the poor cormorant."

We're all silent for a second remembering the poor cormorant. We'd been nursing him back to health under Mal's guidance when he succumbed to a heart attack, from "too much bloody attention," Mal said. That was the suspected cause of death anyway; we never knew for sure as Dad refused to authorize a postmortem. I drew the bird after he died, laid out with his ragged wings stretched to their full breadth, as wide as Alex was tall. His snaky neck and cold eye made a haunting corpse.

Something about the timing of Hope's reminder welded Kit Godden to the cormorant in my brain forever, the golden boy and the ragged black bird. My grandfather's 1954 edition of *British Birds* called the cormorant "a sinister, reptilian bird, often confused with a shag."

Hmm.

Hope sat down. "Well," she said. "So that's it. Shall we drink a toast to summer?"

Everyone picked up a glass except Alex, whom Mum fixed with such an icy glare that he slipped into the grass under the table and stayed there.

Eight voices chorus as one. "To summer."

5

It was three days before Kit and Hugo Godden arrived at the beach. No one over thirty seemed alarmed by the coming apocalypse, but Mattie spent every spare hour on a crazed program of self-improvement. The rest of us drifted in as she applied an oatmeal mask and messed with her hair in the mirror.

"How disgusting," said Alex. "I'm downloading some bats to show the new boys." He considered this fantastically generous. Who, after all, didn't like bats?

"They won't like bats," Mattie said.

"I bet they will. I bet they're starved for bats out where they're from."

"What about Batman?" Tamsin giggled.

Alex ignored her. "If they like bats, they're OK. If they don't, they can just leave."

I shrugged. "Seems fair."

"Batman!" said Tam, louder this time in case we didn't get it.

"Would you all shut up and get out of here?" Mattie's nerves were frayed. She had her mask to remove and her pout to perfect, and time was running out.

"We can take a hint," Alex said, and slammed his laptop shut.

"She's insane," Tam said once we were out.

To Alex this went without saying. "God, I hope they're not the kind of drooling morons who like boobs."

"Boobs, Alex?" Mal emerged from the shed carrying a toolbox. The gate needed fixing.

"The California dudes. I bet it's going to be all boobs and tongues this summer. Revolting." Alex gagged.

"Don't jump immediately to tongues and boobs, young sir." Mal found Alex fantastically amusing, as did we all. "No need to anticipate the worst."

"There better not be." Alex stomped off.

"Can I have a ride to the barn?" Tam gave Mal her most winning smile.

He waggled a screwdriver at her. "Some of us have jobs to do."

Tam sighed and followed Alex into the house.

"Just you and me, I guess," Mal said, draping one arm over my shoulder. "Fancy a bit of hard manual labor?"

"Nah. Think I'll go for a swim."

"You go," he said. "Be free. Enjoy youth's bright dream."

I rolled my eyes. "Yeah."

"Before you know it, you're old and decrepit and hardly anyone wants to marry you."

"I'm telling Hope you're desperate."

"You do that, my love."

I walked down to the water's edge and waded in. It would make a change having strangers around for the whole summer. Good change? Bad change? Alex was right: weeks of flirting and drooling over Mattie in tank tops was more than I could bear. Maybe at least one of them would be sane.

I plunged in and let the icy sea close over my head. Too many thoughts swirled around in air. At least here was silence.

When next I ran into Mattie, she looked retouched: burnished and buffed, her skin tone even, her brows shaped into a clear arch, her legs (and Lord knows what else) hairless with a slight sheen of oil. She smelled of geranium and roses, which we all recognized as Mum's perfume. "I'm just borrowing it," she said, but how can you borrow perfume? It's not like you can return it.

She lay on the big old sofa in the living room, her legs over the back, staring at her phone as if a genie might emerge if she rubbed it.

Mattie and I generally ignored each other, having little in common. It was simpler than jousting over which of life's choices were worthwhile, as none of hers were (in my opinion), and vice versa.

The hours passed as they did the rest of the year, until whatever it was we were waiting for commenced.

6

The morning Kit and Hugo Godden arrived at the beach, Mal was playing cards with Mum, Tamsin was off at the barn with her pony, Mattie was painting her nails, and Dad, Hope, and I were swimming. Gomez was lying in the shade of the back garden, panting and dreaming.

We all saw the car: a long black Mercedes with tinted windows. Not exactly usual around here, so we knew.

I mean, we didn't know the details. What we did know was that they were coming to spend the summer with Mal and Hope, and frankly, what could cause more unadulterated ecstasy than that.

Mattie was as excited as she's ever been. Action at last.

I was suspicious as ever. Why us? Why here? Weren't they old enough to spend the summer on their own? Didn't they have friends in LA?

Tamsin was genuinely in love with her pony and not as susceptible to the possibility of romantic adventure as the rest of us. But even she threw a couple of squares of hay into Duke's box and headed home when Mum texted her.

We converged all at once, Mattie (nails still wet), Mal from our house, Tam screeching in last on her bicycle.

Hope, Mum, Dad, and I were already there.

Summers were spent in swimsuits under T-shirts and shorts, so we looked like a down-market presidential reception committee: scrappy, sunburned, and utterly outclassed. The driver of the Mercedes wore a dark suit and tie, and Florence Godden emerged from the front passenger seat as if stepping onto a red carpet, the white silk panels of her tunic floating round her like pennons. Gomez raced up, ears flapping, but to give Florence credit, she just removed one long crocheted glove, crouched down, and patted him until he lost interest and went back to whatever nothing he was doing.

She was fiftyish, slight, and slightly gaunt in the way of fading Hollywood beauties, dark hair perfectly styled, skin a glistening bronze, huge white sunglasses, features arranged on a grid. The expensive layers of silk flowed over long crease-free white trousers that pooled atop white platform sandals. The sandals appeared to weigh more than she did.

Mattie gazed at Florence Godden in wonder. A genuine movie star, albeit one whose career had peaked long before Mattie was born.

"My darling," sighed Florence at the sight of Hope, "how long has it been?"

"Too long," Hope said, smiling, and embraced her godmother.

"How wonderful to meet you all." Florence spoke with what sounded like a native English accent buried in a faux Texas drawl. "I see *at once* that my boys will be happy here."

The attention of the receiving line shifted suddenly, as if following the ball in a game of tennis. Kit climbed out of the back seat and Mattie's expression shot into focus, something we hadn't seen in ages. For one thing, she almost never found herself the second-best-looking person in a crowd, so meeting Kit must have been a shock. Mattie was accustomed to admiration, having just the right amount of curve, length of leg, largeness of eye, and generosity of mouth to cause men and women of all persuasions to stop, look once, look again.

But Kit Godden was something else—golden skin, thick auburn hair streaked with gold, hazel eyes flecked with gold—a kind of golden Greek statue of a youth. He wore an ancient white polo shirt with an alligator on the left breast, baggy khaki shorts, and flip-flops. His longish hair sprang from his head like Medusa's snakes; occasionally he raked it backward with his fingers.

In my memory he seems to glow. I can shut my eyes and see how he looked to us then, skin lit from within as if he'd spent hours absorbing sunlight only to slow-release it back into the world. His voice was golden too: low and intimate, not squabbly and peevish like ours.

Kit Godden turned his gaze on each of us in turn, smiling a smile full of light. There was self-assurance in his voice, in the requirement that everyone lean in a little to hear him.

Mattie was introduced first, and Kit solemnly offered her his hand. I expected a flash of lightning from the collision of hot and cool, or an earthquake at the very least. Within four seconds he had charmed her practically to death.

The excitement at the center of the group fizzed over.

"Hugo, my darling, where are you?" Florence bent over the Mercedes and removed her sunglasses to search for her second son in its farthest dark corner, finding him and grasping his wrist so he emerged at last, brown and rather plain-looking. He unfolded himself from the back of the car, slightly hunched over, taller and thinner, not athletic-looking like his brother. He wore a plain blue T-shirt and jeans with white sneakers. Nothing else: no fancy cardigan or jacket or baseball cap, no sweatshirt with a logo. His face seemed slightly out of focus, his hands shoved deep in his pockets, his head turned away from the world so it was hard to get a proper bead on him. He looked bony and awkward, with big elbows and knees, like a young greyhound.

You could see his relation to Kit, minus the charm, minus the glow, clearly the runt of the litter, undistinguished except for the scowl and the impression he gave of wanting to be somewhere else.

"Come in, come in," Malcolm said. He led everyone inside and offered drinks while Hope locked arms with Kit and Florence, looking uncharacteristically smug.

"A lot of names to remember," Hope said in a low voice to Kit. "But you'll get it."

Kit went back over the names, pinning each of us

with a knowing smile as if fabricating some not-quite-proper mnemonic.

Malcolm and Mum disappeared into the kitchen, leaving Mattie to gaze at Kit, and Hope to set the table for lunch. Dad and Florence chatted like old cronies; Florence had her hand on Dad's arm, her tinkly film-star voice pitched in the upper registers like a Frenchwoman's. Mal fetched wineglasses and poured an Italian white that hit everyone smack on an empty stomach and made Mattie start to sway, requiring a quick steadying hand from glorious Kit, and a sympathetic smile, and a look on Mattie's face as if her eyeballs might actually melt.

Over her shoulder, Kit glanced back, catching my eye. Poker was more my game, but I could see at once that he could see at once that I . . .

Let's just say that in that moment he slipped between my ribs like a flick-knife.

He held my eye slightly too long, then dipped his head and gazed at each of us in turn.

Oooh. The room holds its breath.

Exhales.

"My beautiful boys," said Florence, taking Kit's arm, gazing at him lovingly and looking around for Hugo, who'd installed himself in the darkest corner of the room, glowering.

We disliked Hugo at once, descending as one into a chorus of judgment on the Godden family—Kit, with every exquisite quality, and Hugo, well . . .

Hope poured more wine and Mattie separated Kit out from the crowd, working like a sheepdog, nudging him gently down the beach toward our house.

"It's nicer than it looks," I heard her say, and he murmured something appreciative in return.

Nicer than it looks? It looks amazing.

"There's tennis and swimming and sailing, and horses up the road, and fishing, and town's just a few miles away, though I don't suppose you drive." She trailed off, a bit stuck for where to go next.

"If I don't like it I won't blame you," Kit said. "And I've got monologues to learn for my Royal Academy audition. So I won't be bored."

"It's not usually boring," Mattie said. She sounded ridiculous—though it was perfectly possible that Godden primo might find his life here insufferably dull. "I suppose it depends what you're used to." And then, "You're applying to RADA? That's so cool."

They sat on the edge of the deck in front of our house and I got a good look at Mattie's betrothed. He had a touch of the ambisexual about him, but you can never be sure with actors. Something about the way he

32

posed with his chin slightly tilted up for the camera gave the game away, as if he'd carefully studied the most advantageous angle for sitting.

"Your house is amazing," Kit said.

"It's been in the family forever," said Mattie, swinging her legs. "We hardly notice it."

Alex stuck his head out from under the porch. "You must be Kit."

"Yes, I must be. Who must you be?"

"Alex." Hauling himself free of the crawl space, he straightened up, blinking in the sun and brushing the leaf mold and cobwebs off his arms and legs. "Ow," he said, stretching his arms up and back. "Cramp."

"What are you doing under there?"

"Checking out the wildlife." He held up a small flashlight and shone it directly into Kit's eyes. "Toads, newts, bugs. All sorts."

"I'm not very good at biology."

"It's not biology," Alex said with contempt. "It's the world."

Kit blinked.

Mattie now: "Do you sail?"

"A bit." Kit followed her eyes up the beach to where a small collection of masts swayed in the lagoon.

"It's tricky getting into the estuary but you get used

33

to it," she said. "You've got to come in much closer than you'd think was safe." Mattie swung her legs in circles.

Kit looked interested. "You'll have to take me. I've only sailed on the Pacific. It's different."

"A whole lot bigger, for one thing," Alex said, and disappeared again.

"We've been coming here for, like, generations," Mattie said. "There's lots of stuff that happens every summer. Near the end of August, Dad and Mal go on The Big Sail, around the point. We're not allowed to go 'cause it's all about male bonding, but one year they nearly got cut in half by a ferry and another time the wind was so bad the mast broke." She paused. "And there's a tennis tournament, which is really fun. It's all highly traditional."

"I like tennis," Kit said.

"Mal's the best player, but I'm pretty good too."

Mattie was pretty good. Not fabulous, but not too bad. We all played a version of kamikaze tennis that avoided rules and took into account the fact that the net sagged and there was no referee. Whoever argued best usually won the point.

Down the beach, Hope rang a bell. Lunch was ready.

"We'd better go back," Mattie said.

"Be prepared for lunch with Florence," Kit said. "She gets highly emotional at partings. Crying makes her feel like a good mother."

"Isn't she?" Mattie asked.

Kit laughed.

7

I studied Florence Godden the way a wildlife photographer might study ring-tailed lemurs. She had a way of drawing attention that couldn't entirely be explained by fame; if she hadn't been Hope's godmother, us kids wouldn't have had a clue who she was. What impressed me was the way she used her brilliant surface to attract and hold scrutiny, then seconds later to deflect it.

"What are you filming?" was answered with the vague description of a young Serbian director who would soon be a household name, a male lead with multiple appearances at past Oscars, and a screenwriter so famous the entire cast had been sworn to secrecy. Given that no one at the table (with the possible exception of Mal or Hope) could name a single living screenwriter, the mystery seemed pointless. But the result was that you didn't realize till much later that nothing about the project had been revealed. Little as I knew about the film business, I had an inkling it wasn't going to open at Cannes.

Hugo possessed the opposite talent, that of selective invisibility, so your eyes traveled over and past him without hesitation. It was quite a skill when you thought about it.

Kit shone softly beside Mattie, happy to let his mother hog the stage. He didn't need to compete and he knew it. And she knew it. There was pride in her possession of him, and a touch of something else.

Hope was explaining about the wedding—"not a big affair, nothing extravagant, you know me"—while Florence Godden feigned shock and said do *at least* let me buy the flowers, and never *mind* the schedule, the film can just *do without me* if it comes to that.

I somehow knew it wouldn't come to that. Hope caught my eye and I saw she knew as well. It felt almost like complicity but the moment didn't stick.

Dessert came out from the kitchen, courtesy of

Mal—a plum tart the size of a wagon wheel that Hope set down next to Hugo because he was closest, and also to include him in the group. A large jug of cream followed.

Hope held the knife out to him. "Will you slice it, Hugo?"

But Hugo shook his head, and Alex seized the knife, chopping up the tart into twelve ragged triangles.

Florence received hers with a great show of enthusiasm, despite having eaten almost nothing at lunch. None of the tart went either, and eventually Mal slid it over onto his plate.

Coffee arrived, and Florence began to make leaving noises. "If only I could remain among you gorgeous friends instead of flying off to Hungary," she said, inflecting "Hungary" with the enthusiasm you might normally save for "Pyongyang."

"Don't go," Mal said through a mouthful of tart. "Goulash and spuds among the Magyars. Dullsville." He pronounced it "*mod-jars.*"

"What's mod jars?" Alex asked, quite reasonably. No one else cared.

"*At my back I always hear Time's wingèd chariot hurrying near,*" Florence said with a sigh. "But until we meet again, I shall keep each and every one of you in my heart." She clasped both hands to her breast with a sorrowful tilt of the head, then (scene over) drew her delicate cobweb gloves over one narrow wrist, then the other, fetched her hat from the table by the door, embraced Kit, Hope, and Mal, threw kisses to the rest of us, and at the last moment stopped and glanced round for Hugo.

"Hugo!" Mal shouted, and everyone fell silent waiting for him to appear.

But he didn't.

By the time he sauntered back into view, his mother had gone.

8

Mattie fell in love quicker than anyone I'd ever seen. It was the checklist in her head working overtime, ticking off life-partner material against a chart she'd seen online called "How to Know If He's The One" that involved lots of pictures of glowing young things giving each other piggyback rides, picking apples, or having pillow fights.

At this moment, she's talking to Alex, who's trying not to listen, and I'm sketching landscapes from the top of the tower.

"What do you think he's like? Kit, I mean. I mean,

really like? Kit. Kit Godden. It's the best name, don't you think?"

Alex looked at her. "I dunno. It sounds like some kind of animal to me. Like a ferret." He drew up his top lip and stuck out his teeth. "K-k-kit. K-k-kit. *K-k-k-kit.* Definitely a ferret. Which is OK by me. I like ferrets."

"He's not a ferret," Mattie called after the retreating Alex, expecting no response and getting none, and you didn't actually have to be in the room to see her flopping down on the sofa, imagining a summer of complete Kit Godden immersion — swimming with Kit Godden, sailing with Kit Godden, hanging around reading books on the sofa, her feet touching Kit Godden's. After that, a discreet historical blank until she reappeared as Mr. and Mrs. Kit Godden and their beautiful children: Coco, Miles, and baby Wolf.

I guessed it would take about twenty minutes before she got bored fantasizing and started looking for an audience. Mattie is the original tree that falls in a forest.

Fifteen minutes, as it happened, before she leaped up and began casting about for company.

"Where *is* everyone?" she shouted. "Mum?" You could hear her in the tower. You could probably hear her eight miles away. *"Alex? Anybody?"*

I leaned out the window in time to see Alex's head

emerge from the crawl space under the porch. "What do you want now?"

"Do you think he'll fall in love with me?"

Alex regarded her critically, drew up his lip again. "You mean K-k-kit?"

Mattie looked hopeful.

"No."

"Yes, he will, I'm sure of it."

"OK." Alex's voice came from within the crawl space, where he'd disappeared again. "Whatever."

Mattie followed him to the porch, knelt, and peered into the darkness. "You'll see."

"Mrs. K-k-k-k-kit."

I closed the window.

Hope and Malcolm had whisked Mattie's future husband and his brother off sightseeing along the usual route—fourteenth-century church, Anglo-Saxon burial site, secondhand bookshop, ruined castle, historic pub. It was hard to imagine them caring much about our local history, coming from LA where there was none.

"They won't be interested in all that junk," Mattie grumbled. "It's a perfect day for sailing, and the dinghy's just sitting there. Kit could have come sailing with me. Come sailing with me, Alex."

"I'm not going to stand in for your future husband.

We'll be out forever and I've got stuff to do."

"*Please*, Alex."

Sometimes I get a blast of how potent Mattie is. When she wants something, she looks so hopeful, so vulnerable, so astonishingly, heart-meltingly needy, and underneath she's steel. People who aren't used to her huge brown eyes and terrifying will sometimes have brain spasms.

Alex held out. "I have tons to do."

"Come on, Alex . . . we can look for seals!"

You could see his resolve melting. I wanted to call, *Hold fast, Alex!*

"OK," he said, defeated, and trudged off to fetch the sails.

They didn't return till late afternoon, wet, salty, and cross, having argued for hours about who was skipper, why neither of them had thought to bring sandwiches, and later, whose turn it was to hose down the sails, with the result that neither of them bothered.

Dad arrived from town just before they stomped separately up the beach.

Mattie threw her arms around him.

"Hello, Matts. You and Alex been sailing? Did you take life jackets?"

"Yes. What's for lunch? We're starving."

43

"There's ham and cheese," he said. "But it's nearly five. Dinner's soon."

"Make me a sandwich, will you, Matts?" Alex collapsed on the nearest sofa.

"Make your own."

"I came sailing with you, didn't I?" He turned to his father. "Mattie's pining for the new boy."

"She's barely met him."

"Doesn't matter."

Mattie stormed in from the kitchen. "He's nicer than anyone in *this* house."

"Obvs," said Alex.

Mattie crashed back into the kitchen, returning a few minutes later to slam a haphazard-looking sandwich down in front of Alex.

"Thanks you."

Dad sat down next to Alex on the sofa. "Seen anything interesting?"

Alex hauled himself up and reached for his laptop. "Look—latest results of Bat TV. Five species so far." He pointed to images on the screen. "Plus this one, which I think is a Daubenton's, very shy . . ." He froze the blurry, bluish video. "Look at it. Beautiful face, don't you think? They usually live underground. Don't know how this one found my bat box."

Mattie leaned over to look at the picture and shuddered. "Gross."

"Numbers are down this summer. You can tell in the evening just by looking. Hardly any mosquitoes for them to eat."

"Their loss is our gain." Dad stretched. "Your mother and I are going for a walk before it gets late—you kids want to come?"

Alex made a face. "Take Mattie with you, might cheer her up."

Mattie kicked him. "I'm not the one who needs cheering up."

"Hey!"

"OK, enough." Dad turned to me. "Come with us?"

I shook my head.

Mattie stayed behind, pretending to watch a film, but actually she was dreaming of Kit. No one but he knew how she really felt.

Or cared, for that matter.

I wondered whether Mattie was going to start off some big drama to disturb the peace this year. It seemed likely. She was desperate to lose her virginity, and what sort of person would say no to Mattie? Surely not some movie star's kid, fresh off the plane.

Meanwhile, there'd be wedding flowers and dresses

and food to sort out, even with Hope's refusal to fuss. I was guessing that the atmosphere would prove contagious and Hope's betrothal to Mal would make something in Mattie's head go a little bit wild.

Still, every summer needs a theme, and I guess Love and Marriage was marginally better than Death and Despair.

9

Dad always woke first. He went for a swim, jogged two miles up to the shop, came back with a newspaper and bread, made coffee, then spent half an hour looking around for some late sleeper to lord it over. If she wasn't sleeping, Mum joined him for the swim, by which time Malcolm and Hope had wandered over for coffee. Everyone under twenty emerged slowly, one by one, youngest to oldest. It was the same every morning.

The only difference now was that Mattie flounced out of bed earlier than usual, bad-tempered and thick-headed, and instead of throwing herself down onto one of the big sofas and waiting for people to bring her tea, she slipped her feet into flip-flops and flapped off in the direction from which Hope and Mal had come.

Mattie and Kit's romance began under entirely false pretenses, Mattie arriving at the little house pretending to look for Hope, whom she'd just passed on the path going in the opposite direction.

Once there, she settled down to wait for breakfast with Kit, sometimes getting Hugo instead. She didn't have to bother disliking Hugo; he hardly registered.

I liked the fact that she never bothered to stalk Kit. She just turned up. When you look like Mattie, it's easy to show up uninvited for breakfast in a way that's adorable rather than unwelcome. What annoys me most is that it takes no effort to be born beautiful, no hard work, no mental agility, no strength of character. Just dumb luck. And yet it's a universal currency, often mistaken for moral superiority.

If Kit had been looking for an effortless summer conquest, Mattie in her pale yellow frilled swimsuit would have fit the bill precisely. But from the first it was hard to tell what Kit was looking for. That's what made it all so very interesting. To me, anyway.

One morning I heard voices below the tower and stuck my head out to look.

"You say," said Mattie.

"No, you say," Kit said, walking near her but not touching.

"OK. It would be on the beach, of course, up on stilts with windows all round, and a ladder I could pull up if I wanted to keep anyone out—like *you*," she said, looking up and seeing me.

Kit followed her eyes and met mine square-on. What a talent the boy had for holding a gaze. I retreated.

"And a roof garden full of exotic plants with a plunge pool . . ."

A plunge pool?

"And inside a whole glass wall that is actually a tropical-fish tank. And—"

"Wow," Kit said. "That sounds much more exciting than mine."

"It's my dream house," Mattie replied in a solemn voice. "I've always wanted a plunge pool and a wall of tropical fish."

"I'm amazed at how specific your vision is," Kit said in a voice devoid of irony. "Maybe you should be an architect."

"I've already decided on medicine," she said. "What about you?"

"Drama," said Kit. "What else could I do?"

Mattie shrugged. "You'd be great at anything you put your mind to. After all, most of getting something is really wanting it."

I stood a little back from the window and did a quick sketch of the two of them. They had their backs to me now and were headed down the beach. *Most of getting something is really wanting it?* What about playing the violin or brain surgery? Or cancer, for that matter? Most of getting something is (a) having some aptitude, and (b) working incredibly hard to master it, or (c) in the case of cancer, just bad luck. So far, Mattie hasn't had much bad luck, but it's early days.

Below me, Alex hauled himself free of the crawl space and straightened up, a bit unsteadily.

"Hey, Alex."

He looked up.

"How's the wildlife?"

"Pretty good." He turned and pointed down the beach. "What's with those two?"

"Mattie's in love," I said.

"Hmm," Alex said, blinking. "Who knew love could be so boring?"

I thought about this. "Maybe he just wants a piece of her tropical-fish wall."

"Yuk. My idea of love involves intelligent conversation, preferably on the subject of bats. Those two don't have a clue."

I stepped back from the window. Even Tam and her horses were more interesting than Mattie's love affair with her own life. Mum got cross when I said things like that. "You underestimate Mattie. Lots of people seem a little two-dimensional at sixteen. She'll grow out of it."

It didn't matter whether I underestimated Mattie. Everyone else overestimated her, so she came out ahead regardless. Not for the first time I wondered about the perverted values of the human race, how beauty trumps nearly everything, including goodness, money, and talent. On its own, of course, it's useless. A wasting asset. And very possibly ruinous for the owner as well. Even the Mona Lisa must get tired of being stared at.

The grown-ups had emerged from the house and now lounged in the sun drinking coffee. I sat by my window with a pad of paper and some pencils. Eavesdropping.

"Aren't you fed up having them round at yours?" Dad asked.

Malcolm laughed. "Whenever we arrive they're on the floor playing cards or chess or What's Your Favorite Dog. I think Mattie's the sister Kit never had."

"Weren't we talking about how to bring down the government at their age?" Dad looked genuinely puzzled.

Mum frowned. "They're playing What's Your Favorite Dog? Are you sure?"

"Yup," said Mal. "I'm sure. Mattie's is a bulldog 'cause they're so ugly you want to cuddle them and Kit says he's wanted a sheep-pig ever since he saw *Babe*."

"That's not a dog," Hope said.

"Whatever gets them out of bed before noon," said Dad.

"Don't mention bed." Mum grimaced. "Does anyone actually know what's going on? I mean when we're not around?"

Mal shrugged. "It all looks pretty innocent to me."

Dad glanced up the path. "Incoming."

Kit and Mattie were coming back, followed by Gomez, who settled next to Mal and stared at him intently till he gave up his toast.

"Hey," said Hope. "What're you two up to today?"

"Don't know," Mattie said. "Tennis maybe?"

"We're going sailing," said Kit.

"We are?" Mattie looked radiant.

Kit nodded. "Yup."

"Be careful of the tides," said Mal, swallowing a

mouthful of coffee. "You'll have to go soon if you want to get out."

Mattie frowned. "I've been sailing longer than you have, Mal."

"He's practicing for having his own teenagers," Hope said. "Why not take our boat? Everything's there, so you don't have to carry it all up and down."

"You're sure you don't mind?"

"Positive."

"Life jackets!" Dad shouted after them.

I watched them go off together, Mattie wearing denim shorts over her swimsuit with an old sweater of Dad's knotted round her shoulders, Kit with a baseball cap and the T-shirt from some LA band so trendy none of us had heard of it. Mattie's hair was turning eleven shades of gold in the sun, and the salt made it wavier than usual. The two of them looked like an ad for expensive sportswear.

Mum glanced up and noticed me watching. She waved. "There's a sign in the shop in town saying they need part-time help. You could apply."

"Really? When did you see it?"

"This morning."

"Hey, Hugo." Mal moved over for him to sit down.

"Hi," I called, and he looked up at me in the tower, said nothing, and turned back to Mal.

I ducked back inside my room before someone could call me down to keep Hugo company. No way was I spending my summer holiday in one-way conversations. I slipped downstairs and out the back door, picked up Dad's bike, and set off at speed.

When I got to the shop, the notice was still up.

Lynn, who owned the place, has known me since before I could walk so could hardly ask for references. I already knew where every item in the place was. Baked beans, fire starters, greeting cards, cheese, onions, vodka. Shelves and shelves of sweets and energy drinks. She wanted me from two to five, three days a week. Short hours, crap pay, cash in hand. I figured money might come in handy if I ever managed to leave home.

Lynn showed me how to use the till. I did some shelf stacking, quite a lot of sweeping, and finally spent a happy half hour going around with a little gun that reads labels and tells you if the food's out of date.

I cycled home.

As I skidded into the drive, I could see Mattie and Kit about fifty meters out to sea, Mattie at the helm, Kit hanging on to the mainsail. The wind had dropped almost entirely, and the sail luffed like a big empty plastic bag. I could hear snatches of laughter. They'd be out there for hours.

I watched for a while, but Mattie had her back to me and Kit was behind the sail, so I wandered off to Malanhope to tell them about my exciting new career.

Mal was delighted. "All the greats started with shelf stacking."

I looked at him. "Alfred? Alexander? Catherine?"

"Not those Greats," he said, waving a hand dismissively. "The industrial giants."

"Rockefeller? Henry Ford? Steve Jobs?"

"Sure. What I mean is, it'd be good if someone around here made a living."

"Excuse me," Mum said. "Some of us work bloody hard . . ."

"Including me." Mal gave us four different emotions in a row, as if caught in a strobe light.

"Hmph," Mum answered, which could well have meant *Get a real job*.

By the time Kit and Mattie got the boat back in, we were halfway through dinner and they had to squeeze together into a single chair at the end of the table. Mattie hooked one leg over Kit's and they ate like that, twined up, sharing bits and pieces from each other's plates, whispering and giggling. Mal and Dad were manning the barbecue or they'd have put a stop to it. As it was, I caught Hugo staring at them with dead-eyed loathing and Alex stuck his fingers down his throat and made gagging noises. Mum told him to cut it out and Hope pretended not to notice. It was a joyless meal for the rest of us, the sense of general camaraderie wrecked. And then, just when I thought I'd get up and take everything back to the kitchen to escape, Kit met my eyes with a smile so knowing, so self-mocking, that I couldn't help smiling back, just a little.

His game, his rules.

10

The shop was never really busy but I liked the regular ripples of arrivals: tourists from the campsite down the road, riders tracking manure across the floor in search of Polo Mints, locals buying frozen meals.

"Have you got any mozzarella?" The woman asking was polite and somewhat diffident, but it didn't charm Lynn, who could barely suppress a sneer. "Or parsley?" asked the woman with fading hope.

"Not today," Lynn said in a tone that unmistakably declared *Not ever.*

"Sorry," said the woman. "Thank you." She seemed ashamed to have admitted to liking something so humiliatingly middle-class as pizza cheese, and I wanted to tell her the shop in the next village sold mozzarella *and* Parmesan. And fresh ricotta and olive oil imported from Italy and homemade cinnamon buns and spanakopita and sausages they made themselves. And parsley.

Lynn didn't like summer people, despite the fact that they spent more money than locals. Her other part-timer, Denise, agreed. I was firmly ensconced in the enemy camp, but had special dispensation due to being cheaper to hire than anyone else who'd answered the ad.

Most of the people who came in, locals or imports, knew me by sight. *Hey*, they'd say. Or *Wotcha?* And boys of a certain age almost always asked whether Mattie was here, unless they were horsey, in which case they'd tell me they'd seen Tamsin.

Of course they'd seen Tamsin. If they'd been anywhere near a horse, they'd seen Tamsin lugging buckets of water from the hose or cleaning tack or taking beginners out for their first rides on lead ropes. There were always five or six girls her age, their sexual development arrested by saddle soap, dedicating every waking hour to pony care.

Like other parents of horsey girls, our parents sighed and paid for endless gear and lessons, telling themselves that horses were a nice safe pastime and at least they didn't have to worry about her joyriding around the countryside with a car full of underage drunks.

This made me wonder if they'd paid any attention at all to the horse world.

Two summers ago, before Tamsin's first show, I walked past a young girl brushing her pony's tail and before I could blink it kicked her square in the chest with both metal-shod back feet. I can still hear the awful thud. It must have broken all her ribs but I never found out because she was taken away by air ambulance. Another time Tam was waiting her turn at a jump when the boy ahead got his stride wrong and somersaulted over his horse, landing in a crumpled heap on the other side.

There were broken bones that summer, a spiral tibia fracture and a separated shoulder. There were concussions and sprains and a teacher kicked in the face by a new livery. The staff seemed to take it all with a measure of benign indifference but the injuries horrified me, as did the size and power of the animals being led around by troupes of fearless infants. Tam would probably have been safer joyriding in the back seat of a dodgy Corsa.

Once on the way home from work I stopped at the barn and caught Tamsin at the end of a long day, drinking tea in the office with the other pony girls. I envied their solidarity, the endless conversation on subjects no one else cared about, the sense of belonging. She always looked happy.

"Don't bother," she told me when I said I might like a few lessons. "You don't have what it takes."

What it takes?

I protested, but she stuck to her verdict and for all I know may have been right.

The job at the shop gave my week a bit of structure, and I appreciated the money. I intended to go to art college and move away from home the minute I finished school — not because I hated my parents particularly, but because I found living with so many opinions and so many competing streams of anxiety exhausting. Exams, sex, body image, food, grades — someone was always in crisis. Sometimes in a big family you needed to claim something to make a mark. Eating disorder, anxiety, narcissism, ponies. Anything would do.

Mal was on the phone ordering a hog roast when I got back from work. He told us he'd always wanted a hog roast. I'd always wanted a Celestron NexStar computer-driven telescope to see into deep space, but a hog roast? He'd found someone to do it for the wedding and now I could hear an edge of panic in his voice.

"Could you hold on a minute, please?" He put his hand over the phone and hissed at me. "Do we want a Saddleback, Tamworth, or Sandy and Black pig?"

I stared at him. "You're going to kill a pig to order? They're practically as smart as we are."

He went back to the phone. "Could you tell me which is most delicious?"

There then came a long explanation with lots of *uh-huh*s and *oh*s, and in the end he said he'd get back to them and hung up. If it had been me, I might have asked which seemed least human or had lived the happiest life.

"I've changed my mind," he said.

"No hog roast?"

"No hog roast. You're right. It's a horrible thought. Maybe I should buy the one they were going to kill and keep it as a pet. Would that make me a better person? Or just an annoying hipster?"

I shrugged. "You've done the right thing," I said. "Let your conscience guide you from here."

"We could give it a name and take it to the park with Gomez," he mused. "I hear they're easy to train. Maybe Hope wouldn't mind."

"Kit wants a sheep-pig."

He sighed. "OK. No pig."

Hope had chosen a date for the wedding at the end of August, based on when the chapel was available.

Chapel?

"I know, I know," Hope said. "Neither of us is exactly godly, but where else are we going to get married? On a fishing boat? In the town pond?"

"How about the beach," Malcolm said, "barefoot with flowers plaited in your hair?"

Hope ignored him. "The chapel on the estuary is perfect."

She was right. It had started life as a lookout tower for marauding Vikings about a thousand years ago, only turning into a church tower as an afterthought. A lookout tower seemed way more appropriate to their union.

"And it happens to be beautiful," Mum said.

No one else wanted to get married that day, so they were in. Mum planted sweet peas for the bouquet and said there might still be roses if we were lucky.

It was obvious that Mum would make Hope's wedding dress. Not that we ever let her make our clothes, but she's actually brilliant at anything from a Yeoman of the Guard with acres of gold braid to Ophelia in a plain white smock. She and Hope were in the next room talking dresses. Hope, in fact, was talking, and Mum was listening.

Half an hour or so later she went off to her studio and, after rooting around for some time, returned with a bulky package wrapped in faded brown paper. Inside was a softly folded pile of blue-gray French linen she'd been keeping for something special.

"How wonderful," Hope said. "I'm going to look like a lovebird."

"A pigeon more like," said Alex.

It was such a beautiful color, like the sky before sunrise, and Hope held the linen up under her chin so we could see how it looked. The dress Mum drew had a full skirt with lots of soft pleats and a scoop-neck top. It was so simple and elegant that we all just sighed.

Hope said at least she wouldn't look like some freakish plastic doll, which was unlikely for all sorts of reasons. She has long legs and what people call a womanly figure, with broad hips and a big chest, not to mention wide expressive eyes and piles of thick dark hair. She moves gracefully, which Mum says is key.

"You should have seen the soprano I had to dress once," she told us. "Body of an angel, gait of a three-legged dog."

Alex, Tamsin, and I stayed to watch Mum take measurements and drape fabric and then take photographs, and Tam said it was just like *Project Runway* and why couldn't she have a dress like that, and Mum said, "Because you're fourteen," and Alex added, "And you stink of horse," which was fair enough, but Tam chased Alex off shouting and three minutes later we heard Malcolm's car pull out, and Mum and I looked at each other and both thought: *Stables*. Tam always managed to get lifts up to see Duke with appeals to non-immediate family like Mal. He said he didn't mind, but I did; no one gave me a lift to work every time I was in a bad mood.

I liked hanging around Hope's house just listening to the talk and preparations for the wedding. Hope wanted trestle tables set up in the garden decorated with wildflowers and plain candles in jars. If it rained, we'd all have to cram into the house, she said, or just stay outdoors with umbrellas. We'd done that before, dinner all set up on the table when the rain starts and no one wanting to shift the whole production indoors. "Only English people would eat outdoors under umbrellas," Dad said, but we didn't see what was wrong with it. The idea that there might be whole countries where you could count on summer weather didn't ever occur to us.

Hope bought a notebook and marked pages out for *Guest List*, *Menu*, *Drinks*, *Decorations*, and *Technical Details*, like the chapel. She filled the pages with bullet points in her small neat handwriting, resisting all Dad's attempts to create a spreadsheet and "organize it properly, for God's sake."

There was something soothing about a wedding, a confirmation that Victorian social order hadn't completely broken down, that it was possible to find your soul mate and live happily ever after like in some cheesy rom-com, unlikely though it seemed.

Hope asked if I wanted a cup of tea but I didn't, so I headed home.

In the kitchen, Alex was editing a bat zombie film on his laptop. "So we meet again," he said.

"Yup," I said.

"KABLAM!" he shouted at a zombie bat, and I went upstairs.

11

I'd only been working in the shop a few days when Kit made his first appearance, wobbling up on Mal's ancient bike to get a packet of rice and some lemons for Hope.

"So, this is your office," he said.

I was at a distinct disadvantage, sprawled on the floor with my date gun, marking down yesterday's baked goods.

I felt momentarily sick with surprise. My hands shook and I was relieved when he turned his attention to Lynn, who was eyeing him while pretending to stack egg cartons.

"Could you please direct me to the rice?" He had on his good-boy voice, without the suggestive undertones.

I scrambled to my feet, knowing that crumpled and foreshortened wasn't my best look.

"I'll show you," Lynn said, which was not her usual policy, and led him to a shelf, from which she pulled a plastic pouch of instant-cook rice. She handed it to him with a pleasant expression, which was also not her usual policy.

He accepted it graciously, though I could see him searching the shelves behind her for basmati, brown, arborio, organic, anything.

After he paid he appeared by my side. "I have new respect for your career prospects," he whispered very close to my ear.

"Yeah, right," I said, trembling a little despite myself.

"No, really," he said, his lips almost touching my ear. "There's something about this whole setup that's strangely arousing."

"Just bugger off," I said, but he was already halfway out the door, grinning.

Lynn and Denise tried to be casual but they knew he was Florence Godden's son, and besides, you didn't even have to be a movie star's son around here if you looked that good.

"So, what's he like?" they asked, and I didn't say he was a mind-fuck who haunted my dreams. I just kind of shrugged and said, "He's OK."

Which didn't satisfy them almost as much as it didn't satisfy me.

After his first visit I waited every second of my workday for the next, but I knew he wouldn't come till I got tired of expecting a visit and stopped waiting.

The only other interesting part of my job was noticing who from the village came through the door, and whether they were with a person they shouldn't be, or maybe buying something they shouldn't. After a while I could read people's entire lives by the contents of their wire basket or what they took to the post office window. Some people spent the whole week's budget on energy drinks and sweets. One guy bought three pizzas a day.

Then there was the post office. Alice down the road returned an average of nine packages a week to ASOS, so we figured she was a shopaholic, and everyone knew she could barely afford milk. Another woman was supposed to be on a strict diet or the hospital wouldn't approve her gastric band. She bought cabbages, onions, carrots, and Weight Watchers bread, but sent her kids in just before closing to stock up on Doritos and chocolate.

When I got home from work, I found Mum in the kitchen threading kebabs onto skewers. Dinner was the big event of the day. Everyone spread around the beach between sunrise and sunset but we all migrated back home for dinner. You had to be careful though; wander anywhere near the kitchen and you were roped in to help.

Tamsin arrived a few minutes after I did.

"Good day, sweetheart?"

Like you had to ask.

"Amazing," Tam said. "I took Duke out on the cross-country course."

"See anything exciting?"

"Two hares, young ones. Just where I saw them last time. One's head is nearly black, so I'm sure it's the same one."

"I hope you were careful."

"Course I was."

Uh-huh.

Alex arrived, tossed some onions in the air, and juggled for about three seconds before they all dropped and rolled around the floor.

"Alex!"

"Saw a bunch of horses I didn't recognize," Tam

69

said. "It's pony camp. The tents are up in the back field."

Mum nodded absently. "Pass me the big platter, please."

"You know they're trapping birds up behind the pig farm."

"Are they? How do you know?"

"I ride back there sometimes."

Mum looked at her. "There's a bridle path through the pigs?"

"It's not exactly a bridle path. I sort of strayed onto it by mistake."

Horses hate pigs. Even I know that.

"You be careful. The farmer doesn't like trespassing. Especially on horseback." She collected one of Alex's onions from the floor. "What sort of bird trapping do you mean?"

"Larsen traps. The wire ones. I saw a bunch of magpies flapping away in there. It was horrible."

"You'll be in big trouble if the gamekeeper finds you skulking around."

Tamsin stuck her chin out. "I wasn't skulking."

"OK. Dinner in half an hour?"

But Tam wasn't finished. "Apparently the magpies peck the eyes out of baby pigs. That's why they catch them."

70

I looked at Tamsin. "Are you sure? Pecking out a living eyeball doesn't seem the easiest way to get a meal."

She shrugged. "They also land on live sheep and eat the maggots out of wounds. Then when the maggots are gone, they keep on eating. That's what Dolly says and her whole family are farmers."

"Cool," Alex said. "I bet eyes are nice and chewy. Yum-yum."

"You're disgusting," Tamsin said, and went upstairs to change her clothes. Tam never helps — does bugger-all, in fact, except saddle and unsaddle ponies.

Malcolm and Hope strolled up around seven, looking freshly showered and clutching a huge bowl of salad from their garden. Some distance behind, Gomez trotted to keep up, panting as usual. Just as he reached them, he stepped on one of his ears and executed a spectacular flip. With a little yelp, he picked himself up and continued trotting with dignity as if nothing untoward had happened.

Kit showed up ten minutes later, and the only people missing by the time food was ready were Tam and Hugo. About five minutes before Mum started serving, Tam came down wearing an actual sundress and Alex pretended to faint. Hugo arrived after everyone had been served, so he got to take home that summer's brinkmanship cup. Go, Hugo.

"Hey, Hugo," I said. Greeting him had become almost a sport.

He glared at me.

Everyone on my side slid down the bench to make space and I found myself crammed up next to Kit.

"You smell delicious," he whispered.

"Thank you," I whispered back. "You smell like a squid."

Kit laughed. Mattie looked daggers at me. Next to her, Hugo appeared ill at ease and droopy. Hope claimed he was better-looking than everyone thought, though not yet, she said, maybe in a few years. I could see he had the Godden cheekbones, a good chin, and large grayish eyes. His uneasy expression wasn't exactly alluring—but still, there was something. He caught me looking and turned away.

Dad fetched another wineglass and refilled Hope, Malcolm, and Kit.

"Glad we all made it," Malcolm said, looking at the kids. "Good day, everyone? No drownings, broken limbs, fatal or near-fatal injuries?" He held his glass up for a toast to survival. "And what about you, Mal? Did you have a good day? Why, yes, as a matter of fact

I did, thank you so much for asking. A very good day indeed."

"Could you pass the salad?" Alex directed this at Dad.

"Please."

"Please."

"Thank you, everyone except Alex, for your kind attention. There's been more reason for me to celebrate today than ongoing betrothal to my beloved. My agent telephoned to announce that I have been invited to perform *Hamlet* at the Rose Theatre." He swept one hand out in a flourish and bowed, at which everyone shouted and applauded raucously. "In addition to becoming a married man, I shall henceforth answer only to HRH the Prince of Denmark. I ask you, does life get any better?"

"Nice to have something to look forward to after the wedding so you don't get too depressed," Alex said, and Mum glared at him.

"Wow," Kit said. "I want to play Hamlet at the Globe someday. That would be amazing." He looked up at Mal. "But the Rose is cool too."

"Thanks ever so much."

Tamsin's expression had turned to horror. "Wait. So you have to memorize all those lines?"

"No," said Alex, leaning right into Tam's face. "He writes them on his arm."

Mal pushed Alex back into his seat. "Four thousand of them. At least one of you novitiates understands that it's not all prancing about onstage in tights."

Kit raised his glass. "To *Hamlet*," he said, and everyone clinked. "Despite all the hard work and Mal's advanced age."

"Thirty-one, matey. Perfect age, in actual fact. Look it up."

Kit raised an eyebrow. Hugo looked bored.

"I did *Hamlet* at school," Kit said. "It was dreadful. Adolescent angst in the home for the terminally wafting."

"The what?" Hope frowned. "The terminally what?"

"Wafting," Kit said. "My school was all about wafting. Girls in silky things wafting hither and thither to classes on poetry and dramatic monologue. Boys wafting after them. Teachers wafting along behind to make sure nobody wafts into drug addiction or teen pregnancy."

Alex giggled. Mum reached over and moved the wine away from him.

Kit stood up. "Like this," he said, and set off down the path, gliding, his head tilted back, his expression demure. Executing a perfect catwalk turn, he wafted back, hands gently fluttering.

"Excellent wafting," Malcolm said. "And Lord knows I've seen some wafting in my day."

Hope looked at him. "I don't waft."

"Certainly not." Mum turned back to Kit. "But you'll be going to drama school?"

Kit shrugged. "What else would I do? Wall Street? The marines? No one in my family's ever done anything useful."

Tamsin was stuck on the number of words in Shakespeare. "Did you actually memorize the whole play?"

"*Hamlet*? It was abridged. But even abridged it's way too long."

"You'll go far," Mal said with a snort. "Maybe you could star in the mime version."

The sun had finally dropped below the horizon, and except for pink and orange streaks to the west it was nearly dark. Daisies and white campion caught the last flecks of light, shining in the high grass like tiny beacons.

Dad disappeared into the house, returning with two lanterns. It took four attempts to light the candles, but then they flickered yellow in their glass sleeves, drawing everyone together.

On the other side of Kit, Mattie was transported, leaning against him with dreamy eyes.

Malcolm took the wine from Mum, struggled briefly with the corkscrew, and then offered it round, avoiding Alex.

The night settled and a few pale stars came out.

"Look at the moon," Mum said, and we all turned to watch it float silently free of the horizon.

"Waning gibbous," Hugo said quietly, and I shot a look at him. It just so happened he was right.

We sat for ages, huddled together talking about the sort of stuff you never remember afterward. Hope leaned against Malcolm, Alex lay on the ground smiling, Tam was half-asleep with her head on Mum's shoulder, and Gomez occasionally gave a little snuffling dream woof. Kit and Mattie had their golden heads together, murmuring something we couldn't hear. Mum and Hope discussed food for the wedding, and Dad and Malcolm talked about their annual sail round the point and up the estuary. The Big Sail always took a whole day, but what else was summer for?

Finally Hope stood up. "I'm off for home. Try not to make a racket when you come in. Who's swimming tomorrow morning?"

"Me," Dad said.

"I'll join you," Mum said.

"'Night, then." Hope disappeared in the dark, followed by the low jangle of basset hound.

Alex crawled over to the table and clambered to his feet.

"Anyone want to play cards?" He produced a deck and began to deal in the candlelight.

"I'm in," Tam said. "Kit?"

Kit leaned back so that his chair balanced on two legs, reached forward, and tapped the table in front of him.

Mattie sighed. "OK."

"Hugo?"

But Hugo had stood up. Without a word, he walked to the edge of the deck, clipping Kit's chair as he passed. The chair overbalanced and Kit catapulted spectacularly backward off the deck while Hugo strolled off into the night. Mattie yelped and ran to Kit's side, but he came up laughing and brushing grass out of his hair.

"My brother's a dick," he whispered to Mattie, loud enough for us all to hear.

When I got up from the table an hour later, the game was still going strong. Kit won nearly every hand and Alex, Mattie, and Tam were laughing uncontrollably as I climbed the ladder to the tower. The sky had clouded over and there wasn't much to see, so I trained my telescope down on the table flickering with lanterns, swung forty-five degrees over toward the sea, and found two eyes staring directly up the telescope lens at me.

I drew back in shock. Hugo. It seemed entirely unlikely that he could see me in the dark tower but it freaked me out so much to find him staring directly up into my lens that I dropped the telescope and swung down the ladder. Standing back from the window, I looked out but there was no sign of him.

The game broke up at last and everyone said good night except for Mum and Mal, who stayed talking in the dark. Feeling restless, I crept silently out the back door under cover of darkness, walked down to the water, and stretched out on the sand. I gazed up at the sky and thought about Swift-Tuttle on its 130-year orbit around the sun. For centuries, astronomers had predicted a collision with Earth a billion times more powerful than an atom bomb—big enough to wipe out all human life. It didn't happen. Instead, the Earth passed harmlessly through the debris of the comet's tail each year, causing thousands of shooting stars. The Chinese recorded seeing them two thousand years ago.

How is it possible, I wondered, that you could set your watch by the trajectory of a comet and the path of the Earth through its tail? Like the cogs of a perpetual clock, going round and round forever. It made me feel better about life on Earth, the reassuring order of things: summer, autumn, winter, spring; birth, growth, death.

The night felt warm and I rolled over and lay watching the regular swell of the sea and listening to the toll of the buoy when Kit and Mattie appeared out of nowhere about fifty feet to my right. I kept perfectly still in the dark, annoyed at them for disturbing the peace.

For a while they sat at the water's edge, talking and throwing stones at the sea, and then Mattie jumped up and pulled her dress over her head, her pale body visible even in the dark. She stood gloriously upright, glowing slightly, arms outstretched, then ran down into the water calling to Kit, who I thought hesitated a second or two longer than would indicate complete commitment to the invitation. Eventually he got to his feet, slowly unbuttoned his shirt, then his jeans, pulled them off, and walked quietly into the water. I caught my breath. Mattie had her back to him, the water lapping round her shoulders, and at last he did what was expected, dived in and came up near her, and all I could see was the two of them, heads together, holding on to each other, kissing.

I watched for a while, jealous beyond measure, because is there anything more romantic than kissing in the sea on a warm summer's night?

The longer I stayed, the more I worried that the moon would burst out the clouds and reveal me snooping, despite my complete lack of premeditation, so while they were otherwise engaged, I went back up to the house.

Mum and Mal were still outside chatting quietly, the lanterns flickering between them.

"Hey, sweetheart, where you been? We thought Kit and Mattie were with you."

"Down by the water," I said, and then, "Nope."

"Maybe they're with Hugo?" Mum frowned. "Did they all go up to the house?"

As if.

"Doesn't matter," Malcolm said. "They're young, let them be. We were young once, weren't we?"

"Don't remember," Mum said, and yawned. "Think I'll go to bed." She looked at her watch. "If you see Mattie, tell her to come home."

Mal poured the dregs of the bottle into his glass and waved good night. I lingered for a second and Mal looked at me, questioning.

"Nothing to see here," I said.

He squinted. "You OK?"

I hesitated. "Fine," I said at last. And went up to bed.

I don't know what time Mattie came home. Mum said she woke at four, went out to the garden house to check, and found her fast asleep in bed, all tucked up in her flowery nightie, safe as milk.

When she emerged at nearly noon, Mattie looked radiantly happy. In some normal romance, this might have been the end of the anxiety-provoking part of the story (the will-they-won't-they cliff-hanger). In this story it was just the beginning.

Later that day, I collected Gomez from Hope for a walk out on the sea barriers. No one else was in evidence, and Hope said, "Mal's learning lines. Poor thing, it makes him so bad-tempered."

There was no way on God's earth I could have learned a whole Shakespeare play in a month and I had no idea how anyone else managed it.

Peering out the window, I could see Mal at the bottom of the garden, pacing back and forth, back and forth, declaiming with extra-added arm movements. I remember him telling us that sometimes while learning lines he had a moment when all at once he realized exactly who the character was and what he was trying to express.

Surely someone must have figured that out already about Hamlet.

12

Mal no longer walked Gomez every morning, so I took over the job. Gomez greeted me in indolent fashion, lifting his head an inch or two off his bed and then dropping it back once he'd checked for edible offerings. By the time I'd had a chat with Hope and a piece of toast, he was fast asleep once more, and it seemed a shame to wake him, but I did, saying his name and stroking his ears till he opened one eye, then the other, then rolled up onto his front legs, hauling the rest of him up behind. Being a basset was a noisy, arduous, rippling kind of existence, irresistible to bystanders.

Hope watched, hands on hips. "I think when Mal runs off with a starlet I'll get myself a nice sleek little whippet," she said. And then kneeling down to ruffle his ears, she said, "You're a very silly dog, Gomez."

"He's not silly, he's majestic."

"You can only be so majestic with legs that short."

"Come on, Gomez," I said. "We're not appreciated here." He followed me out, jangling.

I set off along the beach, Gomez following behind at a steady plod. Mum, Mattie, and a reluctant Tam had gone off shopping for bridesmaid dresses and were planning to have lunch in town. Dad was in London; Hugo and Kit were God knows where. Not together, that's for sure.

Gomez and I turned inland at the footpath and trudged along the bank parallel to the sea. The sun had begun to burn and I felt drowsy and light-headed, so I called Gomez back from where he was snuffling around an old rabbit hole, slid halfway down the bank, flattened a spot in the grass, and lay down.

The grass was tall, so no one could see us unless they happened to leave the bank at exactly the same spot; the hot sun warmed the ground and the cold wind off the sea skimmed just over my head. Gomez turned around three times, settled, rolled sideways, and immediately closed his eyes. He had the body of a big dog, and the warm weight of him along my right side was comforting. I looked out to sea for a time through half-closed eyes, then shut them, listening in drowsy bliss to the oystercatchers and terns and the withdrawing *hoosh* of the waves.

"Hey."

The voice came from directly above and I half sat up, squinting up into the sun to see who it was, but by that time he'd flopped down by my side.

"I heard Gomez snoring," Kit said. "Thought I must be hallucinating and then noticed the grass was disturbed. Perfect spot. Mind if I join you?"

"You already have."

"True," he laughed, and stretched out, hands clasped behind his head, ankles crossed, foot touching mine, accidentally or not. "You like a hiding place, don't you? Always just out of sight."

I glanced over but he was looking straight up at the sky. Gomez had closed his eyes again, tail thumping absently.

Kit exhaled. "Nice spot. Quiet."

"It *was*."

Opening one eye, he grinned. "I'll go if you like."

I didn't want him to go. He was lazy and confident

and made me feel as if he'd gone to a great deal of trouble to find me. I am not entirely immune to flattery. Hardly immune at all.

"So," I said after a minute or two. "You and Mattie."

He laughed. "What'd she tell you?"

"Tell me? Really?"

"OK." He thought for a minute. "It's that obvious."

"My parents haven't figured it out, but that doesn't mean it's not obvious."

He smiled at that.

"Do you actually like Mattie?"

"Yes, of course," he said, frowning. "How could I not?"

Where to start?

He turned and looked at me properly now. "You underestimate her," he said. "She's intelligent, ambitious, beautiful . . ." He shoved me a little with his foot. "Just because she's your sister."

Only trying to figure out your agenda, Kit Godden. Is she really a match for you?

"You don't believe me," he said. "You think I'm a player."

"I don't know what you are," I said, which was true, "and I don't care." Which was not.

He closed his eyes, and the sun settled on the fine arch of his brow. Looking at him was like staring at a prism; you saw someone different from every angle. The one definite was that you couldn't stop looking at him. Partly it was the Mattie syndrome: he needed to be looked at so did everything necessary to attract your gaze. It reminded me of carnivorous plants that give off a beautiful aroma or flash bright colors for allure. He looked nice. He smelled nice. I badly wanted to lick his arm.

Neither of us said anything for a long time and I figured the conversation was closed. But just when my mind had started to drift again, he said, very quietly without opening his eyes, "Which doesn't mean I don't think you're amazing."

My eyes shot open.

"It happens to be true."

Ecstasy and outrage. "You *so* are. A player."

"Have it your way." Kit yawned, stretched his hands above his head, and smiled. "Doesn't mean you're not amazing though."

I tend to trust my instincts, though they're not always right. I explore my fingers for restlessness, the back of my neck for tingle. I can feel when my hackles rise, when something shouts danger. Or when I'm feeling flattered and special and awash with well-being.

At that moment, I felt flattered and special and awash with well-being. While somewhere in the distance, a red light flashed.

13

"Has anyone seen Hugo?" Mal was feeling guilty, as we all were, at how little attention he'd paid to Godden the Younger. To be fair, it wasn't entirely for lack of trying.

You want to play chess, Hugo? You want to go swimming? Go to the shop? How 'bout a walk? Come help with dinner? You want to read a book? It's a good book, you might like it.

The answer was never yes, and really there's only so much rejection a person can take.

"No thanks," he'd say, or just "Nah," or nothing at all, sometimes accompanied by a shake of the head, like he was allergic to social contact, allergic to fun, allergic to us.

Mattie opined that he was socially awkward, couldn't mix, was too snooty and too much of a freak, and it was a shame about him coming along as a package with Kit. Though we all knew where she got her propaganda. Mum and Hope said he was just shy. Dad took the guy road, the not-noticing-what's-in-front-of-your-face approach.

"Hugo?" he'd say. "He seems nice enough."

Uh-huh.

The relationship between the brothers disturbed me. We four fought like beasts but only for ordinary stuff—possessions and food and attention. Hugo and Kit seemed genuinely to dislike each other, though Kit made a joke of it. Hugo didn't. Whenever Kit entered a room, Hugo got up and left.

I watched Hugo sometimes when he was visible, but there wasn't much to see. Sometimes he walked down to the sea. Sometimes he went inside. Sometime he sat on the edge of the deck with a book. Sometimes he just lay on his back on the sand and did nothing at all. Most of the time you couldn't see him. Cloak of invisibility. Other end of the beach. There were so many ways to lose yourself around here. I wasn't interested enough in

Hugo to spend hours wondering about him, where he was or what he did all day.

I tried drawing a picture of Gomez asleep in the grass, choosing him because he was the only live subject likely to stay still for any length of time. I'd been working for ages, concentrating so hard that I didn't notice I had company sitting ten feet away.

He cleared his throat and I looked up.

"Well?" said Hugo.

"Well *what*?" He was so bloody weird.

"You have a strange way of looking out for your sister."

"What are you talking about?"

"I'm talking about the fact that you're getting quite cozy with my brother."

"I am *not* getting cozy with him."

He looked at me and snorted.

I didn't want to be having this argument. "We're friends."

"Friends?" He gave a little mirthless laugh. "Kit doesn't do friends. He does sex."

"Not with me he doesn't."

Hugo shrugged a little.

"You don't even know me."

"Nope." He shook his head. "Don't need to."

A case of sibling rivalry? Hugo jealous of his brother's . . . everything? I didn't blame him. I would be.

"What are you doing here anyway?"

"I'm drawing you drawing Gomez," he said, and I saw that he had a tiny sketchbook and a pen. And I thought, *What sort of idiot sketches in pen?*

"Let me see." I held out my hand, rude, abrupt, and felt surprised when he didn't hesitate, just walked over and handed me the open page. The sketch was scratchy and eccentric but also funny and accurate.

"I didn't know you could draw." The more I looked at the little sketch, the more I saw in it. It made me obscurely angry. "I can't draw like this."

He shrugged again. "You draw how you draw."

I flipped through the rest of the sketchbook. There were portraits of all of us—immediately recognizable pictures that made you laugh and cringe at the same time. And tiny landscapes with unexpected elements: a flying tortoise, an obscene fossil.

"Oh." I felt wrong-footed on the subject of talent and annoyed that he hadn't bothered to reveal it before. There I was, going around making a show of sketching and talking about going to art school and he shows up with a notebook filled with stuff like this. Drawn in pen.

"This is so typical of you," I said.

He seemed genuinely taken aback. "What?"

"You didn't tell us you could draw."

He stared. "You didn't ask."

"You know what I mean."

"No," he said. "I don't." He studied his hands for a moment and I was surprised to see they were trembling. I couldn't read his expression, which wasn't surprising because I could never read his expression.

"Have I done something to offend you?" he said at last. "You act fairly sane with everyone else."

"Offend me? As a matter of fact, yeah. You have. You hate it here. You don't talk to anyone. You creep around—"

"Creep!"

"Yes, creep. Like you'd rather be on death row than here. You don't even like Hope or Mal. All we're trying to do is have a nice summer. You're like the bloody snake in the Garden of Eden."

He gaped at me, outraged. *"I'm* the snake? Oh, perfect. I bet you all wish I was more like my brother."

"I'm not going to say that."

"How very polite." His voice was icy. He stood up, snatched his sketchbook back and stormed off. I felt like stamping my foot in frustration. I'd never met such an infuriating person.

I went after him. "Why do you hate it here so much, anyway? You hated it even before your brother hooked up with Mattie."

He appeared shocked. "I have nothing against Mattie. She's fine."

For a minute I thought he might burst into tears. We were both trembling with emotion. Neither of us knew what to say.

"Look," I said at last. "Let's just forget it."

He shook his head.

"Come and draw with me sometime."

"That's what I was doing today."

Oh for Christ's sake. *"Another* time."

"I don't know." He looked at the ground.

We stood in silence, Hugo flushed, blinking back tears.

"Let's go for a walk."

He hesitated.

"Come on," I said, but he didn't move, so I reached out for his arm.

He flinched, violently. "Don't grab me!"

"I'm sorry, Hugo. I didn't realize you hate being touched."

"I don't hate being touched." He was nearly shouting. "I hate being grabbed."

Right. Fine. A stroll through a minefield, you are, Hugo.

We walked in silence up to the salt marshes. It was so quiet, you could hear the squeaky wings of waterbirds as they flew over. Half a mile. A mile. The tension dissipated, leaving the soft *bosh* of the sea, beeping birds, and occasionally the faint far-off buzz of voices.

"How about here?"

It was a good place, hemmed in by reeds and clouds. A tern flickered above us. I sat down and Hugo followed, a little distance away. A rainstorm swiveled on an axis out at sea, moving away from us.

We drew for some time.

"Pssst!" I heard.

Hugo held up a little sketch, barely more than a few lines, and when I squinted I saw that he'd drawn me, sitting among the reeds. A long arrow rose from my inked heart up toward a tiny bird, its wings blurred.

I looked from the drawing to his face, but the sun was behind him and I couldn't see his eyes. Just for a second, quick as a blink, I felt a little tug of desire. I watched him, the way he held himself back, waiting.

Under scrutiny he dispersed, like smoke.

I didn't sleep well that night. I kept thinking of those drawings. Subtle, funny, perceptive.

And the person who drew them?

14

Mattie was surfing a wave of bliss. After her first midnight swim with Kit, the two were inseparable for about a week. They walked everywhere together, sat pressed together at meals, held hands while reading or eating, and generally made everyone sick.

I spent a lot of time that summer observing Mattie and Kit. You have to understand that there's not a whole lot to do at the beach; summer's not exactly hectic. Having known Mattie all her life, I could tell exactly what she was thinking: *Kit Godden wants me to be his girlfriend. When we're in our thirties and I'm a microbiologist discovering a cure for childhood cancer, he'll be starring in Pinter in the West End, and we'll be the most interesting couple anyone knows.*

I felt a bit sorry for her, which wasn't my usual take on Mattie. I had to think hard to explain it, but maybe I knew that she and Kit weren't playing by the same rules.

Also, maybe I was jealous.

Mattie and Tamsin pranced around the beach in their new bridesmaid frocks, despite Mum telling them it was asking for trouble to wear them before the big day. Both of them looked fancier than Hope in identical white ballerina-style dresses, strapless with stiff tulle skirts. Not Mum's idea of elegant. Tam's had to be taken in to stop the top from falling down; there wasn't much there to hold it up. It was nice of Mum to buy the bridesmaid outfits. She could have whipped up something much nicer in a weekend for a tenth the price, but this made them happier.

At dinner that night Kit said something close to Mattie's ear that made her shove him in mock protest, but he'd already tucked his fingers inside the waistband of her shorts, and she squeaked as his hand disappeared up to his wrist.

"Not at the table, for God's sake," Mal said, disgusted.

Alex nearly choked. "It's happening," he said. "Just like I said it would. The summer of *tongues*."

"Calm down, me hearty," Mal said. "If they don't stop public displays of affection I'm going to run them through with a lance. You can aid and abet."

After dinner you'd stumble on them entwined together on a sofa or trip over them on the beach or find them crammed into the hammock you wanted to lie on. There they were, head to toe, Mattie's bare feet neatly pressed up against Kit's rib cage.

So had I just imagined my conversation with Kit? It was just one line, after all, one word, *amazing*, couched in a careful double negative. "Doesn't mean you're not amazing."

He thinks I'm amazing—as he lies tangled up in a hammock kissing Mattie's perfectly shaped, slightly sandy bare feet. He thinks I'm amazing—as he sticks his hand up the inside leg of her shorts and she squirms mock outrage.

Maybe he didn't mean amazing. Maybe he meant *fine*. Maybe it was an aesthetic judgment, a sort of "Someone else will like you someday" kind of comment. But that's not how I remembered it. I remembered it with the connection between his eyes and mine, with the shrouded invitation that (may have) accompanied the words.

One thing about Kit Godden, he did know how to construct reality in his own image.

At this he was clearly no amateur. He'd smile, talk, make jokes, throw his arm around my shoulders, all in a perfectly friendly, slightly impersonal way until I was convinced I'd imagined the words, or maybe not the words—the intonation, the implication that amazing meant amazing. And the instant he saw me ready to spit out the hook, he'd give the line a little tug, and hey presto.

I thought about what Hugo had said, about Kit and sex. With all the gaslighting going on, at least I could reassure myself that he didn't just want to be friends. That he found me sexually and intellectually alluring enough to consider as a lover. Didn't he?

After a few days, by sheer force of will I stopped thinking about him and went back to things I wanted to do. I even dared, after midnight, to do a quick sweep of the beach from my tower, terrified and expectant that I'd see him skulking back to the house pretending he wasn't having sex with my sister.

But there was no sign of Kit or Mattie, or anything else interesting for that matter. Until at the other end of the beach I passed something unfamiliar, went back, focused, and once more found myself looking directly into Hugo's eyes.

What the hell?

I lowered the telescope and with my naked eye saw a figure standing a quarter of a mile away, facing me, but much too distant for me to see, or for him to see me for that matter. He was certainly too far away to have any clue that I was looking at him. This time there was no doubt about it. No lights on in the tower, no possible way a person could even know I was awake.

Picking up the telescope, I lifted it cautiously. He was still there, his eyes trained directly on mine, as if standing a few feet away. He could have been in the same room staring straight at me. It freaked me out.

Did he stand staring up at the tower twenty-four hours a day on the off chance that he might catch me looking out? It didn't seem likely, somehow.

As I watched, he walked back up the beach and disappeared into Malanhope's. The house was dark.

Was I going crazy? Was he?

I coined a new series of collective nouns. A plague of Goddens. A murder of Goddens. A conundrum of Goddens. A siege of Goddens. A pounce of Goddens.

A chaos of Goddens.

15

The wedding was taking shape. Alex was happy with his bats. Mal obsessed night and day about *Hamlet*. Tamsin was forever in love with Duke, and Mattie with Kit. Kit seemed to like Mattie back. Mum was sewing and Dad was doing whatever it was he does all day. It was all as boringly predictable as if Tuesday had decided to follow Monday.

And then Kit became elusive.

If you could be bothered to draw a graph, you'd see Mattie's passion continuing to curve upward like the GNP of India while Kit's stalled somewhat, like China's, giving every indication of tailing off and heading downward over the coming fiscal period.

You might even say that Kit began erring ever so slightly on the side of aloof.

This set off a reaction that involved Mattie spending most of the morning trying to run into Kit, failing, then returning to the house to try on five different outfits, each as adequate as the next but none precisely right enough to compensate for the empty feeling of not being with him. Having chosen one, she'd spend half an hour brushing her hair into a ponytail that looked casual but wasn't. Once she'd gotten the hair right, she'd realize the shorts were wrong, then the shoes, storm into the kitchen in trainers and run out again, return in flip-flops, then barefoot, in ballerina flats, flip-flops again, over and over as if shoes were the key to Kit's heart and if she could only decide on the exact right pair he would love her the way he had last week.

Only he wasn't playing the shoe game. One day he didn't show up for lunch or dinner. Headache, Hope said. Poor boy. And Mattie didn't look just disappointed, but deflated and gray, like she'd been punched.

Then the next day he had work to do. And the next he read all night, so he slept for most of the day.

The following night, when Kit did show up,

Mattie avoided him, sitting with Alex on one side and Mal on the other. But it didn't work because she hadn't reckoned with the puzzled look, the hurt look, the why-are-you-shunning-me look, the I-will-undermine-any-confidence-you-have-in-your-own-instincts look. That last look turned her into the sort of girl who doubted the evidence of her own moderately competent brain.

Sometimes I caught him looking at me and I felt a flash of triumph. He'd tired of her, just as I'd known he would. Now all I had to do was wait.

The more agitated Mattie grew, the more Kit screwed with her, "forgetting" that they were supposed to meet up, arriving late, going off for long walks with Mal ("With Mal? But why didn't he ask me?"), or inviting someone else along, someone who had no idea he was being used, like Alex. And then just when Mattie was starting to feel so angry and upset that she might stop caring about the self-obsessed ghosting bastard, he'd show up with his fatal smile, his burning eyes and soft low voice, and he'd put his arm around her waist and nuzzle her neck and say, "Where have you been?" when it was perfectly obvious where she'd been, given how hard it was for him to avoid tripping over her.

That's when Mattie's excuses began. "If you had his mother, how would you be about relationships?"

and "You might not believe me but he's weirdly innocent about women." That was harder to believe because Kit was many things, but innocent didn't appear to be one of them. "He's not like other boys," she'd say. "He lives in his head." Or, scathingly, to me or Alex, "You wouldn't understand someone as sensitive as Kit."

"Did you ask him why he didn't show up last night?"

Mattie looked away. "No."

"Why not?"

"I can't."

"Why can't you?"

"I just can't. Anyway, no one's really supposed to know about us."

Everyone within a fifty-mile radius knew about them.

"Why not?"

"Isn't it obvious?"

I thought about this for a minute. "No," I said.

But she just shook her head and walked away, and I was left feeling bemused that over the space of a few weeks, Mattie had been transformed into a person who couldn't ask Kit why he didn't show up when he said he would.

I, on the other hand, increasingly found myself on the receiving end of his attentions. Nothing concrete, no groping in the pantry or guilty kisses on the stairs. But whenever I looked up I met his eyes, and whenever I made some comment under my breath, he alone managed to hear it and huff a short laugh.

I am aware of you, his attention said. *I'm interested.*

And then there was Hugo, exactly his usual polite, withdrawn self, not really talking to anyone, just managing to be there and not there. Our drawing expedition hadn't tipped us over to friendship, but he and I had achieved a momentary truce, and there seemed a possibility of building on it.

He appeared at the house one afternoon when I was doing not very much and at first he just stood there, like a ghost.

This is your chance, Hugo old boy. *Hello* would be a good start.

"Hello," he said, his usual brilliant conversation opener.

"Hi." He didn't follow up, so I took another turn. "What's up?"

"Your mother wants someone to pick samphire for dinner."

Anyone else on the planet would have added, "You wanna come?" but not Hugo. The amount this annoyed me was disproportionate. I waited, saying nothing. The silence seemed to go on forever.

"You wanna come?" he said at last.

"Sure," I said, like rewarding a dog for figuring out what "Sit!" means.

Hugo turned to go without waiting for me and I sighed. We headed out across the salt marsh, him leading, a canvas bag with scissors flapping by his side. The tide was out, so we had no trouble finding the stuff and no trouble reaching it, though the mud climbed up over my ancient flip-flops and dragged the rubber stems through the holes with every step. I gave up and took them off.

Pulling up a particularly toothsome branch of samphire, I offered it to Hugo.

"Put that back!" He was outraged. "You don't pull up the roots, for God's sake."

I knew that, but he was the only one with scissors.

"Why don't I hold the bag," I offered pleasantly.

He shook his head in disgust, squatted down, and started snipping carefully. "They won't grow again if you pull the roots out."

"They've been growing here as long as I can remember. Anyway, what exactly do you know about samphire?"

He glared at me. "California isn't the moon. We have plants."

"Sorry to underestimate you."

Hugo snorted. "Why stop now?" he said, and we were back to square one.

He cut samphire for some time in silence, handing me the bag eventually and then the bundles, which I stacked carefully. It was not a strenuous job. I found a moderately dry place to sit. Neither of us said anything for some time.

"Are you OK?" He asked this without looking up.

I blinked. Why did everyone keep asking me that?

"Why wouldn't I be?"

"Lots of reasons."

"Like?"

He sat down, hooked the scissors on one forefinger, and swung them round and round. He didn't look at me, just watched the scissors.

"Well?"

"Nothing. Just be careful."

He was talking about Kit, obviously. But I was

careful. And anyway, I knew something about Kit that Hugo had no way of knowing. I knew how he behaved with Mattie, that he wasn't serious. Anyone could see that.

And I also knew how he looked at me.

16

After another forty-eight hours of avoiding Mattie completely, Kit appeared at ours for breakfast with Gomez and Mal, slid in across from her, and slowly unleashed the Godden smile. Mattie flinched as if he'd hit her and I could feel cold uncertainty pooling at her feet like blood.

But Kit was just starting.

Slowly, like a gymnast warming up, he joked and cajoled, made eye contact and broke it, found her eyes again and held them, went serious for a minute, laughed, smoldered. I could tell that something was going on under the table too. Slowly the color returned to Mattie's cheeks and she started to forget the misery of the past few days. I watched her release and soften until once more she was his.

Just like that.

But I could see traces in her eyes of hesitation. The *Did I just imagine that?* look I recognized so well. And I hated seeing it, how pathetic it looked.

None of the responsible adults noticed what was happening because Kit didn't want them to notice. He made sure to pay exactly the correct amount of attention to Mattie when other people were around so the mental manipulation stayed their little secret. And if those three words don't make you shudder, you're not having the correct reaction.

They agreed to a walk after breakfast, and Kit talked about camping out on the beach in Malcolm's tent while Mattie listened, eager as a spaniel for everything to be perfect between them once more.

Mum joined us with coffee and seemed delighted at the warmth of the atmosphere. She and Dad had this cozy idea that Mattie and Kit were still getting to know each other, in a sort of old-fashioned way, maybe holding hands sometimes on the beach or talking into the night. A great deal more was happening but only when Kit was in the mood. Or maybe when it was so dark that he could close his eyes and pretend she was someone else.

The question was who.

Hugo arrived, perching on the end of the opposite bench like an animal who might need to flee at any moment. I made a genuine effort to catch his eye, but he refused to throw it and I felt like hurling a fork at him. Why did I even bother?

Eventually Mal got up and said he was going to buy a newspaper and did anyone want to come, but Mattie and Kit didn't even notice. Mal ran his hand up and down between them to check if they were blind, but they ignored him.

Hugo said, "I'll come," and followed Mal out, and it was the first time we'd actually seen him volunteer to be sociable.

I got up to leave too, only to be waylaid by Dad with that big-eyed pleading look you see on the faces of baby pandas.

"Tamsin's competing today and I promised I'd help her with Duke."

"Great," I said, and turned away, entirely not in the mood. "Have fun."

"Oh, please," he said. "Please come. You know what I'm like with horses."

He looked so hangdog, and of course I know that you have to play with your parents sometimes to keep them from feeling unloved, though I'm ashamed to say I normally can't be bothered. I sighed and followed him to the car.

"What a gorgeous day," he offered as an opener, but it didn't work for me because (a) I wasn't interested in the weather, and (b) I was so baffled by various Goddens that it had, frankly, been a pretty shite day so far. Weather notwithstanding.

"Whatcha thinking?"

I sighed again and glanced at the sweet, guileless face of my father.

"Nothing," I said, not wanting to upset him with the Byzantine goings-on in the teen underworld. "Just wondering if I can remember anything about pony prep."

"The important thing is to be there for Tamsin. You know how she gets."

Yes, I know how she gets. She gets blamey and panicky and freaked out, and if her pony's toes aren't shiny or his mane isn't plaited just right, she bursts into tears and stays there. I don't know how I got sisters like mine. I bet my dad doesn't know either. Neither he nor Mum is a narcissist weirdo.

We pulled up at the yard, and there were about a zillion ponies being groomed by a zillion little girls. It smelled of horse manure, grease from the burger van, and, underneath it all, the stink of performance anxiety. This is where it all starts, I thought, the anorexia, the self-loathing, the control-freakery. *My pony's not as nice as that pony. We knocked down a pole. Must work harder. Must go faster. Must jump higher. Must grow up and marry a banker to support my expensive taste in extra-curricular activities.*

There were a lot of bankers' kids in the practice arena, and I felt a slight pang that Tam was so outclassed on Duke, who's kind of a dirty chestnut and well past the first blush of youth, but when we found them he looked glossy and alert, his mane and tail plaited, all his tack buffed and gleaming, and Tam in immaculate white jods and black boots and stock tie. They looked good.

"You're gorgeous, darling," Dad said, and kissed her, which was the wrong thing to do because she'd just managed to get her hairnet absolutely straight and didn't want to be disarranged.

"Help me with my number," she said through gritted teeth, and he tied the bib carefully over her jacket. I held Duke's head while Dad gave her a leg up, and then I said good luck like I meant it. For Duke's sake I wanted her to win so she didn't insist on upgrading to some shiny new model. For a moment I felt a rush of longing for the good old days when we all rode scrubby bad-tempered ponies who never did anything we asked. This whole new performance element seemed wrong, fun-free, and somehow anti-pony.

We waited with Tamsin by the warm-up arena, and when they called her number Dad gripped the rail and shot me a look that said, *Here we go!*

Duke knew his job and when Tam got her approach wrong he adjusted his stride so smoothly she didn't even notice. I kept thinking she'd forget the order of fences, but she didn't, and Duke went round like a champion, jumping clear. Tam was radiant, leaning over to hug and kiss Duke's neck as they left the arena.

"Good boy!" she said, and I thought, *Well done, Tamsin, still in love with your pony, no issues with you.*

No one else went clear, so there was no jump-off, praise Allah-Jehovah-Zeus, and after Dad delivered the requisite well-dones and I'm-so-proud-of-yous I nudged him and pointed at the car. He glanced nervously at Tam, who was leading Duke back up to his box, and shrugged.

"Let's risk it," he said, and we escaped, laughing like schoolkids.

It's a short drive home, and as we came round the corner toward the beach, we almost hit a figure walking on the verge with his back to us and his thumb out. Dad slowed.

"It's Hugo," he said, and pulled over. "Hop in, Hugo."

I wish he hadn't just said, "Hop in, Hugo," like Hugo was Skippy the Kangaroo.

"Hello," I said in what might have been construed as a somewhat aggressive tone of voice. "Hello, hello, HELL-O."

Hop-in-Hugo looked slightly panicked.

"How are you enjoying your summer, Hugo? Settling in?" asked Dad, as if Hugo were a box of cereal on a shelf.

"Fine," answered Hugo nervously.

Another silence. Longer this time. Awkward. But I was done with making all the effort.

We passed our drive and Dad stopped at the end of Malanhope's.

"OK," he said in an overly friendly voice. "Mind if I drop you here?"

Hugo hopped out kangaroo-style. "Thanks for the

lift," he said, and closed the door without a backward glance.

"Seems a nice boy," said Dad.

A nice boy?

I smiled and nodded kindly to protect him from his own tragically flawed lack of insight.

17

Mum was working on a jacket to go with Hope's outfit. She wanted a slight swing in the bell shape and was sewing stiffeners along all the seams so the linen wouldn't flop. The jacket was more difficult than the dress because it was tailored, and she kept running down the beach with it draped over her arm to check the fit.

I was just coming up from a swim when I saw her leave the house, so I waved.

"Come and see it on," she called, and I wrapped the towel round my shoulders and followed her. Hope was in a striped T-shirt and jeans when we arrived and looked so much like a hopeful eighteen-year-old that it was hard to imagine her ever getting married.

"I don't even like dressing up," she muttered as Mum helped her into the jacket, adjusted the shoulders, and pinned the side seams.

"Now you tell me," Mum said.

Even though the outfit was complicated to make, it looked simple on, like a child's idea of a party dress.

"And," said Mum through a mouthful of pins, "it fastens — like this." She tucked the ends under a spare strip of fabric and held it up to the jacket.

Hope looked at herself in the mirror. "Pretty," she said without smiling.

Mum nodded. "Where's Mal? I haven't seen him all day."

"In hiding. Learning lines. I think he might have dragged Kit in to play the rest of the parts. I'd help him, but he won't have it. Says I give him disapproving looks."

"Do you?"

"Probably."

"Last seam," Mum said, and Hope sighed.

"I won't have a decent conversation with him till the run is over. Maybe I should get pregnant. Make your own best friend."

"Don't even joke about it," Mum said, frowning.

"What's wrong with children?" I asked. "Your life isn't blighted."

"Get a cat," she said, ignoring me. "To keep Gomez company."

"He'd love that."

Gomez, hearing his name, padded over and flopped down on the floor next to me like a sack of hammers. I scratched his ears. "Would you like a cat for company, my darling?"

He didn't answer.

We heard the back door open.

"Greetings, fans." It was Mal.

Hope smiled. "You look quite cheerful for the son of a whoresome queen."

"Remorseless, treacherous, lecherous, kindless villain! O, vengeance! Though this be madness, yet there is method in it! What a piece of work is a man! I must unpack my heart with words and fall a-cursing like a very drab, a scallion!"

We looked at him.

He paused. "Not a scallion. A scullion. Just testing."

Kit entered the room after him, threw his arms out, and struck a pose. "Fie upon't! Foh!"

"Foe? What foe?"

"Not foe, f-o-e. Foh, f-o-h."

"What on earth is *foh*?" Hope laughed.

Kit shrugged.

"More." Mal crossed his arms and waited.

"Don't tempt me. I could do the whole play tomorrow."

"Go on then."

"Wouldn't dream of showing you up, Malcolm, me bonny Scottish swain. But I am ready to step in at a moment's notice should you require a more age-appropriate Hamlet."

Mal rapped him on the head. "Ah, callow youth."

"I like *remorseless, treacherous, lecherous villain*," I said. "I'm going to use it on Alex."

"Alex, lecherous?" Mum looked at me.

"Remorseless, then."

"Try it," Kit said, grabbing my arm and pulling me to my feet. "Declaim. You can make it up as you go along."

"No."

"Go on," said Mal. "Here, I'll start you off. Fie! Ye treacherous, villainous whelp of a whore . . ."

"Thanks," said Mum.

Mal looked at her. "No offense."

"None taken."

He turned his gaze back to me.

"No."

"*Come on.*"

"Go on," Hope said.

I sighed and struck a half-hearted pose. "Begone, forsooth, afore I strecken ye entrails to a pulp. O Romeo, thou black-hearted knave, that is the question, me hearties."

Mal looked pained. "What was that?"

"Pirate Shakespeare," Kit said, nodding admiration. "Very modern."

"It was your idea."

"Pirate Shakespeare?" Mal frowned. "I don't think so."

I shrugged.

"Whatever it was, don't make a habit of it," Mal said, his eyes lighting on Hope. "Is this the sacred garment of our impending nuptials?"

"You're not supposed to look," Mum muttered from under the hem. "So bugger off and stop looking."

"Come on," he said to me, "let's go and declaim a game of tennis. I've got to clear my brain by murdering someone."

"I can't play like this."

"Then go and get changed and meet me over there. Come on, chop-chop."

"Hang on, I'll come and watch," Mum said, gathering up the panels of unfinished jacket that Hope had carefully removed. "I'm finished for now."

"Thank you for being a saint." Hope hugged Mum.

"Can I borrow Dad's racket?"

"What's wrong with yours?"

"Broken string."

Mum shook her head. "Why does everything in our lives always need fixing?"

I took this as rhetorical.

Mal murdered me at tennis, which cheered him greatly. Mattie was mooning around when I came in the door.

"Hey, Matts."

"Hey," she said. "Seen anyone around?"

"Anyone in particular? Just played tennis with Mal. Hope's at home. Mum's probably upstairs. Alex? Tam? Hugo? Nope. Kit? Last seen with Mal. What happened to your walk?"

She didn't answer, just dropped back on the sofa facedown with her head buried in pillows. So the roller coaster was heading down once more. The high-low cycle seemed to be speeding up.

A bit later, when I did my usual afternoon beach survey, I spotted Gomez lying on a nest of towels, watching Malcolm, Kit, and Mattie in the sea. Mal was swimming parallel to the shore in a lazy front crawl, while Kit floated farther out, blowing streams of water into the air. Mattie paddled nearer the shore, where she could catch the waves just before they broke. Every few seconds she glanced casually out toward Mal and Kit, though neither paid her much attention. She finally gave up hoping that Kit would swim back to her, and set off in a casual breaststroke toward the deep water, where she floated with the boys, bobbing and swooping the swells.

You could pretend all you liked that Kit adored her and pursuit just wasn't his style, but it looked to me as if he was perfectly happy to hang out with her, as happy as he was to hang out with anyone else on the beach, give or take some after-hours action.

I swept the beach from end to end but saw no sign of Hugo.

The sun was warm, even this late in the day, and after Mal et al. went back up to the house the beach was deserted, so I walked down to the edge, looked around quickly, stripped off, and stepped in. Swimming naked in broad daylight is a good incentive not to linger. The August sun sparkled on the sea. Big black cormorants stood out on the sandbars, arms outstretched, drying their ragged feathers in the sunshine. I ducked my head and held my breath, then came up so that only my eyes floated on the surface, and glided along on the border between sea and sky, my body suspended below, like a crocodile looking for prey.

I couldn't see another soul in any direction. Existence distilled to peace and freedom and a sense of waiting in an infinite present.

18

If there hadn't been a wedding planned that summer, it all would have been different. If there hadn't been *Hamlet*, ditto. And if there hadn't been any Goddens, it presumably would have turned out to be just another summer, indistinguishable from the rest.

Would that have been better?

One thing that continued to puzzle me was that we'd heard nothing at all from Florence Godden.

"She doesn't do email," Kit said. "Finds modern technology terribly crass. 'That's why I have an assistant, darling.'"

"Doesn't she ever phone? WhatsApp? Text? It's not like it costs anything." I was drawing a cardoon in black pencil, a glorious four-foot purple flowering artichoke. Kit was reading an Edward Albee play.

"My mother? Only if it occurs to her, and it never does. Postcards, once or twice a year." He peered at me sideways. "You don't feel sorry for me, do you? That would be nice. But don't bother, I don't miss her."

"Never?" I reached for my charcoal.

"Not since I was about six. I hardly think of her as my mother. She's more like some vague relation, a crazy aunt you only see at Christmas."

I shaded the fat stem in vertical lines. "What about Hugo?"

"What about him?"

"Maybe he misses having a family."

Kit shrugged. "I don't know. I don't know much about my brother."

"Aren't you interested in finding out?"

"Nope."

"I'd say he knows a thing or two about you."

Kit grimaced. "He thinks he knows a thing or two about just about everything."

"So I should ignore him?"

It killed Kit not to ask what Hugo had told me. But he didn't. He just shrugged. "Do what you like."

"I think I will."

Kit held out for a few minutes just to prove that he wasn't going off in a huff, then got up and left. He didn't like any conversation that included his brother.

What had happened to cause so much bad feeling? They didn't go to the same school. They didn't live in the same house (boarding schools). The subject of a father was never raised, in itself suspicious. And of course Florence clearly favored Kit over Hugo, which never led to positive sibling relations. See also *King Lear*.

I finished my drawing and went in search of the reviled one, finding him at the little house, on the sofa, eyes closed, earphones in. I tapped his shoulder, resisting the urge to peek at his playlist. He was weirdly private about stuff like that and I didn't want to piss him off.

Hugo opened one eye and pulled an earphone out.

"Hi," he said in what almost sounded like a pleasant tone of voice.

"You want to do something?"

"Like what?"

"I dunno. Tennis?" I knew Kit played; he'd brought a racket with him. Hugo probably did too. Didn't all

Californians? "I'm not great, but I can usually hit the ball."

"Yeah, OK. Can I borrow a racket?"

I nodded and he unfolded himself from the sofa, sat up, and ran his hand through his hair, which had all flattened on one side of his head. "I'll just get some sneakers," he said.

He kind of loped upstairs to his room and came back wearing his flat white Converses. Not great for tennis. I had gel-soled trainers with extra bounce. Very pro. I handed him Mal's racket, which was one of the better ones going, and he spun the racket in his hand, checking the tension on the strings.

We didn't say much on the way over. One of the good things I'd discovered about Hugo was his capacity for silence. In that sense, he was better than almost anyone I knew except Gomez.

When we arrived I told him Mal had taught me to play but that he always beat me. Maybe he didn't teach me the tricks of being a good player on purpose, so that he could keep winning, but it was way more likely that I just didn't practice enough.

"I played some at school," Hugo said.

"Tennis at school? You should see my school. Athletics twice a month if it's not raining, which it

always is, gymnastics, which is a joke, and games, whatever that is."

"We had tennis, yoga, martial arts, and meditation.
Every day."

"Wow."

We warmed up a little, just batting a few balls
back and forth around the court, and he seemed to
be running more than I was, which encouraged me. I
was mostly getting the balls back to him and started
thinking that at least I could give him a decent game.

"You want to serve?"

I shook my head.

"OK."

His first serve was easy and I hit it back into the far
corner, so close to the line that it kicked up a little chalk.
It was a lucky shot, not representative of my skill, but I
could see him frowning slightly, considering.

His next serve almost took my ear off. I barely had
time to lift the racket when it slammed the ground a
quarter-inch short of the line and exploded against the
fence.

I stared at him openmouthed. "Christ, Hugo.
Where'd you get a serve like that?"

He shrugged and served again, a baby serve so I
could hit it back.

I let it go. "Do it again."

I watched this time to see how he did it. He didn't look particularly athletic — his shoulders weren't big and his arms didn't bulge — but when he threw the ball in the air his whole body seemed to coil and then extend like a spring so that when the racket made contact with the ball the force came from his feet and knees and the whole uncurling flow of his thighs and the muscles of his back and shoulders. It was awesome.

When he saw that there was no point playing big-boy tennis with me, he went back to serving softly and hitting the ball more or less directly into the path of my forehand so I could return it and not feel out of control. I was used to losing to Mal, who fancied himself a decent player, but this was something altogether else. Even the sound of the ball on his racket was nothing like mine, which made an average sort of *thunk*. His contact was sharp as a gunshot. I felt almost sick with jealousy and suddenly liked him better. He revealed himself slowly, did Hugo.

We played for an hour and Hugo never broke a sweat. Mostly he carefully returned my shots so I could hit them again. Then at the end of a rally, during which I almost felt I could play the game, he'd casually flick the ball just beyond where I could reach it, so fast I barely clocked it flashing past. If we'd been playing for real, the game would have been over in seconds.

"I'm going to die if we don't stop," I said at last, panting, and threw myself down on the bench. "I wish I could play like that."

"You could," Hugo said. "It's just practice."

"I couldn't practice enough in a lifetime. You make it look like high art. I'm just whacking balls around. It's what we English are best at, you know, losing with grace."

Hugo frowned. "This country's weird."

"You can talk."

A fleeting smile.

We headed back to ours for something to eat and a swim. The sun had been in and out all day. Hugo borrowed some trunks from the line and we finished last night's leftovers, ignored the half-hour rule, and went straight in. The waves were rough, blown sideways by the wind.

"Please don't tell me you surf too," I said once I'd gotten used to the water.

"Nah," he said. "Tennis and swimming. Scuba. Bit of cross-country. Soccer. Basketball." He thought. "Baseball, lacrosse, tae kwon do. Kickboxing. That's it."

I shook my head. "We grew up on different planets."

"I guess."

"So what's LA like?"

"It's OK." He shrugged a little. "I'm used to it. What's London like?"

I had to think. "Noisy, dirty." I swam sideways. "But I like it. It's home."

Hugo was taller; he could touch the bottom. "LA's not home. Nowhere is."

The simplicity of this pronouncement startled me. How could nowhere be home? Home drove me insane most of the time but in a pinch it was everything— house, parents, siblings, friends, school. "What about..." I hesitated.

"My mother? Brother?"

"Your father?"

"What about him? I've only met him twice."

"You and Kit don't . . ."

"No," he said, looking straight at me for once. "We don't. I'm not sure she fucked either of them more than once. Or anyone else for that matter."

Oh.

Hugo dived under the water and I watched him swim two powerful strokes before I lost him in the murky sea. He came to the surface some distance away, caught a wave toward the shore, clambered out, and shook his head like a dog. He didn't turn back, just picked up his towel and headed up to the little house. I watched him go, thinking about what he'd said.

What I'd read as dislike turned out to be something else. Damage?

19

When we were kids, the six weeks of summer holiday felt like an unfathomably deep moat between the end of one school year and the start of the next. But now that we were older, time accelerated, and by the time the rhythm of summer declared itself it was nearly half over. Wedding plans seemed to play into this; when you're running out of time to organize a party it focuses the mind. The boat trip was still to come and the tennis tournament always signaled Nearly September, which made it something of a melancholy event. In the meantime, there was no word from Florence, not even an RSVP to the invitation, which discomfited Hope as she'd figured Florence's appearance would double as a trip to collect the boys.

With unease bordering on dread, I thought ahead to the day Kit and Hugo would leave the beach — Kit by way of London for his RADA audition, Hugo, with his mother, back to LA. Kit and Hugo would hang out with old friends, rekindle whatever relationships they had in real life. With any luck Kit would return to RADA. Hugo had another year left of school.

And what about us?

Kit appeared in the shop again the next day, just as my shift was ending. He said he'd give me a lift home on his bike.

"You're not seriously suggesting I sit on your cross-bar?" But when he leaned in I caught a whiff of salt and sweat and I wanted to breathe it forever.

I started down the road at a jog and he followed on Mal's crummy bike, riding with arms folded across his chest, pedaling slowly and steering with his hips. He started singing to me in Italian, like a gondolier, until I pushed him and he grabbed the handlebars to stop himself crashing.

He settled for rolling beside me with one hand on my shoulder so I did all the work pulling him along. My whole body vibrated under his fingers.

About a quarter of a mile from home he suddenly let go, and without a backward glance sped off as if he'd just remembered the time.

A few hours later, he flip-flopped up the beach.

I was finishing the cardoon, drawing in the spiky thistle flower with a purple pencil. "You disappeared in a hurry."

"Always leave 'em wanting more."

I felt a genuine flash of contempt. "You're joking."

He laughed. "I remembered something I promised to do."

Uh-huh.

No other explanation was forthcoming. "There," I said, and held up the drawing for inspection.

He looked carefully. "I'd like to have that."

"Hands off. It's for my portfolio."

"Will you do me another sometime?"

"Nope."

He ran his hand along the inside of my leg.

"Mmm . . ." he said, and I shoved him hard.

"You are such a slut. It's not Mattie you like, it's anyone."

He looked hurt then. "I adore Mattie," he said. "She's gorgeous. But you . . . you're something else."

"Yeah."

He narrowed his eyes, like a cat. "Something . . . else." His fingers on the inside of my thigh.

I held my breath.

"I think about you," he said, staring up at the sky. "I know I shouldn't but I do. I think about you way too much." And then he turned his gaze on me.

The electricity coming off him could have lit a cruise ship. *Oh God*, I thought. But that's not what I said.

"You know what, Kit Godden? You're a spoiler. You won't be happy till you've ruined my sister's life." I sounded ridiculously dramatic, even to me, like some insane version of the love police.

"Totally unfair," he said, removing his hand from my leg. "I'm not going to ruin her life. I like Mattie, but you're not suggesting I spend the next fifty years with her, are you?"

Well, no, I wasn't. I'd believe anything as evidence that it was me he wanted, not her.

Was it necessary for him to be madly, fatally in love with either of us? Was mad, fatal love the only honest love? On the one hand, of course not. On the other, who set out cold-bloodedly to have an affair without even the hope of real feeling, the kind that might last? Was it just naivete on my part, thinking that's how it should happen?

137

He looked at me, all at once razor sharp, voice low. "There are things I want to know about you. Questions I have." His eyes held mine and my whole body shivered.

"I'm not in a rush," he said. "Aren't you tempted?"

Tempted? Me? That was like asking if I was tempted to get wet in a rainstorm. By the time you finished the question I was already soaked.

I picked up my drawing pad. "See you around," I said.

I walked away. Resolute. Hard. Collapsing.

20

Tamsin got a ribbon in her first jumping class. Mal worked on his lines. Mum finished the jacket. Invitations were answered. Nearly forty were expected for the wedding meal, despite Hope's insistence on an intimate affair. Mal's parents were coming, and his married sister; aside from that it was friends. It would take place mostly on the beach and we'd all cram into the house if it rained. Hope seemed calm enough, reading steadily through a pile of books by her hammock. When you asked if she was nervous, she opened her eyes wide and said, "About what?"

They'd decided on a vegetarian menu despite Mal's longing for a hog, because it made catering for a wide range of eating disorders easier. Hope made a list of ingredients, calculated quantities, ordered a great deal of local wine (English pinot noir, courtesy of global warming) and three cases of French champagne. Glasses came from the winery. Hope hired four local girls to help with food prep and waitressing on the day ("You kids are guests"), and Mum's depthless prop cupboard provided tablecloths for the trestle tables in light green and blue.

"Why is no one making me a wedding outfit?" Mal was half a bottle in.

"I'm happy to rustle you up a little something, Malcolm dear." Mum smiled sweetly at him. "But I'd have to know more about the desired effect."

"The desired effect? Isn't it obvious? Love god, finest actor of his generation, sensitive intellectual, savior of womankind . . ."

Hope didn't even glance up from her book. Mum looked thoughtful. "I'm thinking sky-blue velvet? Matching embroidered waistcoat and . . . sandals?"

"No Panama? Pshaw!" said Mal, filling another glass. "This is exactly why I'll end up getting married in a swimsuit and tweed jacket. Nobody takes my haberdashery requirements seriously."

"I didn't know you had haberdashery requirements, my darling." Hope reached out to stroke his arm, but he slapped her away.

"Don't patronize me. I shall provide my own attire and surprise you on the day."

"Not too surprising, please."

"Righty-ho." Mal turned to Alex. "Can you sew, my good lad?"

"Sew?"

"Wield a needle. Tickle a buttonhole. Let out an inside seam." Mal wiggled his eyebrows suggestively. "If anyone's interested, I dress to the —"

"No one's interested," Hope said. "I think it's time we ate."

Mal took Tamsin's arm and headed for the kitchen. "You'll help me find something to wear, won't you, my dear one? We can have matching outfits. That would make me extremely happy." Tam beamed.

Mattie was the opposite of happy. Nervous, unsure of herself, eating less, and biting her nails till they bled. She had lost weight and it didn't suit her; the sharp outline of her cheekbones made her look older. I, on the other hand, surfed a wave of promise. *When all this is over*, I thought, *I can stop making a stand*. When he's at RADA and I no longer live at home. When life is real. Then, maybe. Then. I could find out how patient he really was.

"How do you think Kit and Mattie are getting on?" Mum was picking thyme in the garden.

Hope shrugged. "They seem reasonably happy to me."

"I'd hate for her to get hurt. She seems completely mad about him."

"It's summer. It'll be over soon no matter what," Hope said.

Mum sighed. "Poor Mattie."

"Oh, I don't know. I'd have killed to hook up with a guy like that at her age. At least he's not forty and married."

"Forty?" Mum blinked.

"It was very romantic at the time."

I'd never heard this story. "Romantic with who?"

"Whom."

"Romantic with *whom*?"

"You shouldn't be listening," Hope said. "My tutor at drama school. It lasted a couple of years. But I was older than Mattie—nineteen or twenty."

"And you met Mal after?"

"I was still seeing the tutor when we met. I kept

both going for months." She looked thoughtful. "Mal grew on me. But it took time."

I hadn't heard this version of their love affair before. "He always says it was a *coup de foudre.*"

"It bloody well was," Mal said, emerging from the house with more glasses.

"For him, not me."

"Oh, thanks very much." And went in again.

"So what changed your mind?" Mum was in reporter mode.

Hope hesitated. "I don't know. I grew accustomed to his face, like the song says."

"That's it?"

She shrugged. "Who knows? Over time, I didn't get sick of him. Plus, he was mad about me."

"Mad about the boy . . ." Mal sang from the kitchen.

"Stop eavesdropping!"

"And then one day I realized life without him wouldn't be nearly as nice as life with him."

"You crazy romantic fool." Mum bundled up her fistful of herbs.

I thought about this for a minute.

"Hey, why the long face?" Mal burst out again and fake-tackled me to the ground, performing a one-sided stage fight with all the sound effects as I tried to roll away.

"Get off me, psycho!" And then Mal was away on *Psycho*, complete with the knife and the shower music, and by the time I crawled out from under the movie montage, I was exhausted from panting and laughing at once. When I looked up, I saw Kit watching us with an odd expression. Mal saw him too and missed a beat, but then was off again, on to Shakespeare mixed with Fred Astaire, doing a sand dance while reciting *To be or not to be*.

Hope shook her head. "Can you believe I'm going to marry that dork?"

Any of us would, given a chance.

21

Going to work was an escape, not just for the change of scene, but to get away from the creeping claustrophobia on the beach. All the fresh air that blew in with the Goddens at the start of summer was beginning to turn stale, and an undercurrent of anxiety hummed through the house. It pissed me off. Summer was for pleasure and boredom, not chaos and doubt.

At work I knew that if Lynn was in a bad mood, it was because there hadn't been enough rain for her garden or her husband had come home drunk again. Denise, whose shift overlapped mine, was twice my age and mainly interested in gossip magazines. It was all very restful.

"Will you look at this," she'd say, pointing to some famous film star, tutting and shaking her head. "Why would anyone hook up with a sex addict? If I had the kind of choice she does, I wouldn't touch him with a barge pole."

Because he was the closest they had to a genuine local celebrity, Denise and Lynn were dead keen on Kit Godden.

Whenever he came to the shop, he shuffled and stammered so charmingly that Lynn always said afterward, "You'd never know he was practically famous himself. So natural."

Kit's version of natural was a carefully constructed illusion. I was learning a lot this summer, most of it stuff I didn't want to know.

When I told Kit that the ladies fancied him, he came up to meet me after work, bought all the newspapers for Mal, *Your Horse* magazine for Tam, and *Country Life* for Hope because she liked looking at stately homes.

Kit talked to Denise for a while about the music festival up the road and all the traffic and inconvenience it caused.

"But doesn't it bring in more business?" asked Kit in a voice that suggested he cared. "All those extra tourists?"

"They don't buy here, just expensive stuff from town and drugs on-site. It shouldn't be allowed." Lynn had her posh voice on, especially for Kit.

"You'll flirt with anyone," I said when I finally dragged him away.

"I was not flirting." He rode his borrowed bike in slow circles around me.

"Jesus, Kit, can't you find someone else to annoy?"

"Am I annoying you?" He smiled his slow smile.

"You are."

"That is not my intention."

I stopped short. "What exactly is your intention? I only ask because every time I see you I end up feeling just . . . so . . ."

I searched for the word. *Humiliated.* Tears sprang to my eyes and I brushed them away with the back of my hand. Part of me knew he would take advantage of genuine emotion to advance his game, and part of me just wanted him so badly that by the time we kissed I had no thought of asking him to stop. We kissed in the middle of the road, him still on his bike, both hands on my shoulders so that if I stepped away he would fall over.

He swung his leg over the seat of the bike and with the hand that wasn't holding it steered me off the side of the road to where the hedge hid the field beyond, and then pulled me down on top of him on the grass and slipped both hands up under my shirt and along the smooth skin of my stomach and it was skin against skin and mouth against mouth and his mouth was . . . Oh, what was I doing?

I knew what I was doing.

I expected urgency but he took his time, controlled matters with a precise sense of what he wanted and where and how. I couldn't breathe for wanting and waiting and finally at long last having. And finding out just how good he was at proving that a person might almost die from wanting and having.

Afterward I lay dazed and waited for my breath to return to normal. I turned my back on him, pulled my jeans up, and hugged my knees, and he touched my face calmly as if something had happened that was now over. But there was no quenching it for me. I yearned like a greedy child. *Again, again, again.*

He was standing now, holding out his hand to pull me up.

What have I done? I asked myself. *What have I done?*

"You," he said, wrapping me in his arms and whispering close to my ear. "You change everything."

I'd waited so long to hear those words that I didn't even care that they weren't true.

22

The next morning I came down late and everyone was somewhere else except for Hugo, who sat facing outward on the opposite side of the deck, long legs dangling, semi-invisible, drawing in his notebook with an old-fashioned pen and a bottle of black ink. He turned when I arrived and caught my eye and in that instant he knew. His expression changed not a whit; there was no flare of disgust or resignation or triumph, just the slightest contraction of the pupils and an extra beat holding my gaze, and then he went back to what he was doing.

Kit and Mattie arrived when I was halfway through

breakfast, followed by Alex, who'd been up for hours and had already eaten, so he didn't hang around. I went on buttering toast exactly as usual.

By now I knew that if I asked Kit how he really felt about Mattie he'd say she was an amazing girl. And me? I knew how he felt about me. I changed everything.

I think that when he said those words he meant them, though perhaps not in the deeper sense of actually meaning them. I racked my brain to figure it out. Was this just what relationships were like these days? Whatever you felt like with whoever was there? I didn't want to look as if I didn't understand the rules.

Perhaps he just needed everyone to love him. Even I didn't need that much love. *Even Mattie*, I thought, *didn't.*

Looking up from breakfast I saw that he was still holding hands with Mattie, drinking coffee with his other hand and watching me with a small smile. When Mattie went inside to get more milk he leaned closer. "Don't think so hard," he said in a voice that caused my whole body to flicker. "I can see your brain starting to smoke."

"Fuck you."

He grinned.

I had stopped noticing Hugo, but became aware of

him again. He got up to leave, carefully screwing the top on his bottle of ink and gathering up his drawings. He didn't look at any of us as he walked past, and nobody much noticed him, so that when he flicked his pen, spattering a comet of black ink across the back of Kit's white shirt, no one saw but me.

"What shall we do today?" Mattie asked, sitting down again.

"I thought I'd go over Mal's lines with him," Kit said. "Hope's right, he's awful at it. Seems the least I can do."

Mattie stuck out her lower lip. "Oh," she said.

Kit grabbed her round the middle and snuffled around under her clothes like a pig till she snorted with laughter and pushed him away.

"Why don't you come along and play Ophelia? You'd be great."

But that wasn't what she was after, and she said she'd rather go into town with Mum.

"I'm not playing Ophelia either, before you ask."

He grinned at me. "Aw, come on."

Mattie hated that he'd nearly asked me too.

"Don't know what you're missing," he said, getting up. And then he wafted off back to Malanhope's.

Mattie had tears in her eyes but she turned away

before I could say anything. And what would I have said?

I went back up to the watchtower and lay on the bed. The day was hot and still; the temperature rose and rose. The beach would have been cooler but I was too torpid to move so I dozed and thought of Kit and his expert cool hands. I knew he didn't feel for Mattie what he felt for me; Mattie was too pretty and simple. He came to me for something tangled, dark, compelling. That's what I told myself.

I heard a quiet knock, so quiet that at first I wasn't sure if it was an actual knock or just someone on the stairs. I got up to open the door, not entirely happy to be disturbed.

Surprise! Hugo.

"What do you think you're doing?" He was angry.

"Why is anything I do your business?"

We glared at each other for longer than was comfortable.

"You should know better," he said at last.

"Oh should I? Shouldn't your brother take responsibility for the way he acts?"

"Obviously."

Obviously? I stood, hands on hips, staring at him. Uncertain suddenly. "What does that mean?"

"He's an asshole. That's what it means."

I stared.

"People fall in love with him. Don't you see?"

I knew that, of course I did, but I didn't want to hear it from Hugo. "Why does what I do matter to you?"

Hugo blinked slowly. His eyes darkened and his whole expression clouded over. "You don't get *anything*, do you?" he asked. "I'm trying to help and if you weren't so *dumb* you'd get it."

His gaze shifted to the wall behind me, where my large drawing of the dead cormorant hung. Hugo stared for a few seconds, then turned and left the room, thrashing blank space out of the way to get through the door. I didn't see him emerge again on the beach. He was either lurking in the kitchen trying to psych me out or had vanished into thin air.

I flew down the stairs. "Hugo!"

Alex looked up from the computer. "No Hugo here."

I felt like stamping my foot in frustration. No sign of him outside the house. No sign of him inside. What was he, some kind of shape-shifter? I ran down the path to Malanhope's but there was no sign of him there either.

"Sorry, darling," Mum said.

"Cake?" Hope held out a plate of apple cake.

I slammed the door and turned toward home,

bumping into Mal coming up from the beach.

"What's up?" he asked, frowning.

"Nothing."

"Talk to me," he said, and pulled me away from the house.

"Fucking Goddens," I said at last.

"Ah."

I shook my head, trying to dislodge words. "Hugo's impossible. I don't know how to be friends with him or even if it's worth trying. Sometimes I think I like him and other times . . . he's just infuriating."

Mal nodded. "And?"

There was nothing I could tell him about Kit. "Kit . . ." I started. And then closed my eyes.

Mal was silent for a minute. "Imagine your mother was Florence Godden."

"No thanks."

"And no sign of a father. Sent away to school, dragged around the world, dropped for months with people you don't know . . . it's not much of a school for relationships."

"Sociopaths, maybe."

Mal raised an eyebrow. "That's a bit harsh."

I stared at my feet.

"What about Kit?"

"What about him?" I could hear myself. I sounded furious.

He peered at me. "Is there something you're not telling me?"

My jaw was welded shut. I couldn't speak even if I'd wanted to.

We walked on for a bit.

"It's like they've set themselves up in opposition to each other," Mal said. "The light and the dark." He paused long enough for me to wonder which was which. "I don't even want to guess how they reached that point." Mal stopped and peered at me. "You're not . . ."

I didn't help him.

"You're not . . . You haven't? Do you want to give me a bit more information here?"

I didn't. Pathetic enough that Mattie couldn't ask why Kit stood her up; I wasn't about to talk about sex with a sociopath in a field.

I sighed. "Everything just feels like hard work all of a sudden. Summer used to be fun."

Mal nodded. "I know what you mean. I'm sorry it's turned out like this." He rested his hand on my shoulder. "But you'll be OK. You're smart and tough and talented." He tried to meet my eyes. "Downright amazing, you are."

To be honest, I'd had it with amazing.

I left him and headed down to the sea. He didn't follow. The tide was out and a handful of people still lingered on the slope of the beach. Hardly anyone was in the water, too scared of riptides or fatal undertows to let their kids in without a lifeguard. I pulled off my shirt and dived in. The shock cleared my head. I floated, bobbing over the waves, then set off down the coast in the direction of the tide with my adequate crawl, keeping it up till I was too tired to continue. The return was much harder and I made almost no progress for ages, at last managing to scrabble up the shelf, exhausted. I stopped in a foot of water to drift, floating and spinning with the waves until I'd rested enough to stagger back up onto the warm sand to dry.

It was the best time of day, when adults drift off home for gin and families set off for supper but the sun still feels hot.

Was any pleasure more perfect than the slow progress from cold to warm?

I lay dreaming of Kit's sure hands and slow smile, and wound barbed wire around my thoughts to exclude Hugo and Mattie.

When people express nostalgia for youth, I always suspect they have inadequate recall.

23

Two weeks left of summer.

"Day after tomorrow's The Big Sail," Dad said, "Mal, Kit, and me. Crack of dawn, around the point, don't expect us back till nightfall."

"Or sober," Mal said.

"How come Kit gets to go and not me?" Alex was furious. "He's not even related."

"Next year," Mal said, but Alex wasn't having it.

"Remind me to grow up to be everyone's lover boy," he said, and stormed off.

But Dad didn't end up going. The stables phoned that afternoon to say Tam was in the ER with a broken arm. Dad and Mum waited hours for an X-ray, which revealed a messy fracture; they would keep her in and operate the next day. Tam was stoic but by morning the waiting and the pain had gotten to her and she cried and cried till they sedated her for surgery. Mum stayed at the hospital while Dad came home for a change of clothes, returning to find Tam groggy from anesthesia with her arm in plaster. Mum was drawn and tired, but after all, she said, it was only a broken arm.

Back at the beach, Mal and Kit decided to go for it on their own because the tides would be exactly right and if they waited for Dad they'd lose the moment. "Off you go," Dad said on the phone, "don't mind me. I'll just borrow some of Tam's meds for merriment."

Mattie made a not-very-aggressive attempt to get invited along in the boat, but Mal fended her off, saying, "This is all about male bonding," and he and Kit each put an arm around her and kissed her till she collapsed laughing, and then Kit picked her up and kissed her again, in front of everyone, which made her so happy she didn't mind staying behind.

I missed the famous kiss but heard about it from Alex, Beach Twitter working overtime to spread whatever news might be of interest to the masses.

* * *

Mal and Kit set out early in the morning on a lee tide through the deep channel. The combination of wind and water sent them off at speed.

"They'll have a hell of a time getting home," Alex pronounced. He had excellent instincts for natural forces, so no one argued. "Kit says he can sail, but I'm not convinced. And Mal's mostly good at being crew. They'll miss Dad. He never gets stuck."

Once they left, everything felt quiet and a little flat. It pointed out with total clarity how much the summer ministry of fun (and intrigue, deception, and sex) depended on Mal and Kit. Without them, life felt strangely empty.

Tam returned home from the hospital late in the afternoon, filling the void with stories of the fall, the ambulance, and a general fury that she was banned from riding for the remainder of the summer. She was expected to be in plaster for eight weeks, with PT afterward to make sure she kept full use of her hand. Nobody thought she would actually stay away from the yard, but Dad threatened such dire consequences that I almost admired Tam in advance for ignoring them. My guess was that she'd be up on Duke again in days if not hours, risking further injury, amputation, or worse.

Dinner was a desultory affair, indoors because it was

already starting to get cold at night and we could all glimpse September peering at us over the far edge of summer. Alex failed to start a card game, Mattie was teary (again), and I stood for some time on my widow's walk looking through the telescope for signs of the sailors' return. I got bored after a while. Not bored, depressed.

It was well after dark when Kit and Mal returned. They claimed to be too exhausted to talk about it.

Too exhausted to talk about The Big Sail? It was unprecedented. The whole point of The Big Sail was the aftermath, the game analysis, the postmortem, the blame: who was completely hopeless at getting the spinnaker up, who couldn't steer a straight line, who forgot to check that the pub closed between three and five.

But there was none of that, or almost none. Kit went straight back to Malanhope's, claiming a splitting headache, sunstroke possibly, though there hadn't been an overabundance of sun. Mal went straight up to Tam's room to offer sympathy, then stayed for a drink and to hear hospital horror stories from Dad. But he was strangely silent on the subject of the day. Dad tried to draw information but got nowhere, and anyway, his past couple of days hadn't exactly been easy. You could see he was tired.

Our clamor for the genuine story just seemed to annoy Mal.

"It was fine," he said. "Hardly the idyll I had in mind. Kit isn't much of a sailor, we had trouble with the tides, and the wind dropped out completely when we got to the point, so we just sat around in irons, didn't make it to the pub until four. It took twice as long as it should have to get back, *and* it rained, *and* once we lost the sun it was bloody cold."

The end.

The sketchy facts of the day were presented in an oddly joyless narrative, not crammed with the sort of hilarious anecdote we expected from Mal, not to mention the combination of Mal and Kit. It's hard to explain how much of a disappointment it was, being the big event of the summer, and how much we'd all been waiting for the story, hoping for tales of man overboard and mutiny—true or invented, we wouldn't have cared.

Mum asked later if we thought Mal and Kit had quarreled, which hadn't occurred to me but might explain the subdued story. Hard though it was to imagine Kit losing his cool, the ever-adorable Mal could be somewhat tyrannical when skippering, like almost every other sailor I'd ever met. And I suppose he wouldn't have mentioned that in his account. I figured the real story would come out eventually, but in the meantime something about Mal's version unsettled everyone.

The next morning was humid and gray, and a generally pissy mood reigned. Another day of clouds and bad temper made me want to hide away, possibly forever, so I went back to bed till early afternoon. Alex kept texting me to come swimming, play tennis, watch Bat TV, make lunch. I turned off my phone.

At last hunger got the better of me. When my texts for Alex to bring up some food failed to elicit a response, I put on yesterday's clothes and went downstairs. It was nearly three o'clock and the house had an empty feel. Nobody was around, a relief at any other time that today intensified the gloom.

There was cheese in the fridge, and bread, and I stuck some of it on a plate with a couple of tomatoes, then slunk back upstairs, climbed the ladder up to the tower, and sat on the widow's walk to eat, looking out.

Even on a gray day, the beach is beautiful. A smooth cover of cloud hung just over the sea like the lid of a sandwich box; thistles, fennel, and broom stood out against the beach and rows of young starlings crowded the phone wires. Across the lane I could see young bulls, eight or so, some lying, some standing and grazing. And far off to the right was the old farmhouse, with a couple of shire horses in the meadow colored gray with mist.

Dog walkers were famously undeterred by drizzle and I could see a few — a solitary woman with a small dog, another with two collies, an older man with a spaniel. Then farther off in the distance two men with something the size and shape of a basset hound.

I reached for my telescope, and though I couldn't make out faces at that distance, it was definitely a basset and definitely Mal and Kit, nearly half a mile away.

I'd barely seen Kit in days. He hadn't even been to the shop for milk, much less flirtation or sex by the side of the road. It was as if our little encounter meant so little to him he'd forgotten all about it.

Where we were concerned, Kit had gone to ground. My stories to explain his behavior made a nice companion volume to Mattie's. Seeing him with Mal, my first thought was relief; Mal would put him straight on any number of sociosexual confusions. Who else but Mal — the elder statesman of youth, with his memory of sex and intrigue still intact? I wondered if they were talking about me.

I watched for a while but there wasn't anything much to see.

One odd result of Mattie's and my shared obsession was an unspoken desire (more on my part than hers) to share space. It puzzled Mattie, who couldn't fathom what we had in common all of a sudden. If there hadn't been years of alienation to fall back on, we might have seized the moment to discover shared interests.

I heard her come in sometime later. It was impossible not to. As lovely as she was to look at, she walked like the Hulk.

I went downstairs, silently, to freak her out.

"Where is everyone?" I asked, and she jumped.

"Don't know, don't care."

Fine. I flopped down on a sofa, pretending to read.

Time drifted as we waited for something to happen.

Something finally did. That perennial wild card, Hugo.

24

Ten days left till the wedding, and all at once I under-stood the danger of giving summer a destination. It became a steeplechase, and no matter how many dramas occurred along the way, all anyone really thought about was the finish.

With that in mind, and the odd atmosphere that no one could quite pin down, we didn't feel much like running the tennis tournament. But it was an annual event of such long standing that no one dared suggest skipping it.

Everyone played, there were no seeds, we arranged

the matches by luck of the draw, and the stakes were about as low as humanly possible.

The only other person who'd played Hugo was Alex, who constantly begged everyone for a game, but who played so badly no one wanted to waste the time. There was some suspicion that Hugo was coaching him, but no amount of coaching could turn Alex into a threat.

Kit had been playing genial knockabouts with Mal and Mattie but his game was more rumored than proven. I had a bit of an instinct, however, not to mention direct experience regarding his general strength and skill. I pretty much figured he could play.

Hugo refused at first to participate in the tournament, but Tam and Alex got on to him and ragged him half to death, and Mum finally took him aside and had a quiet word, which no doubt went along the lines of "We'd really like you to join in," with the emphasis on *really*, in a tone of voice more usually employed in military conscription.

The first rounds were played one weekend, one set per pair, the second rounds took place the following Saturday, two sets plus tiebreak if necessary, and the final was played on Sunday, the following day. The intervening week wasn't for resting; it was just to make sure anyone with a job who might have to be in London could participate, though people with actual jobs were a bit thin on the ground this year.

Round one went like this: Mum played Mal and lost. Alex played Hugo and lost, just, in a game of unrivaled good cheer. Hugo even seemed to enjoy the match, which was practically the first time I'd ever seen him enjoy anything. Alex slammed balls at him at random, failing entirely to hit them about half the time and whacking the remainder all over the place, but Hugo returned them regardless with a great show of effort so that Alex genuinely thought he'd played well.

Tamsin was out of commission, so Mattie also played Alex, who wanted a second chance. Their game might as well have been a boxing match, for all its amiability and finesse, and Mattie beat Alex decisively. Dad lost to Hope in a surprise upset, and that just left me to play Kit.

Tennis, as we know, was not my sport. Sport, in fact, was not my sport. So when I took my place cross-court from Kit, six foot two glowing inches of muscle and stealth, the best I could do was to lose with grace.

I had no intention of losing with grace.

Instead I played every shot like a grenade, aimed at his face, slammed a backhand directly at his crotch, insisted balls were out when they clearly weren't. Days and weeks of sexual frustration and fury guided my hand. There wasn't a single moment during which I thought my tactics might be effective, but I didn't care.

"Whoa, kid," Dad called from the sidelines. "This is not the Wimbledon final."

"Good thing too," said Kit, who hadn't strained to hit a single ball.

It wasn't till I faced him on the tennis court that I realized how angry I was. He looked puzzled and a bit miffed at the level of aggression directed at him, and my anger only grew as I realized he had no idea why I might even be upset.

I lost every point, though he allowed me to play a few rallies to the end, probably just to see if he could keep the ball in play. Lord knows it wasn't fast tennis, and it certainly wasn't good tennis, but his command of the game was so good that a scenario formed in my head to distract me from losing with honor.

I glanced over at the onlookers and caught Hugo's eye. He was thinking exactly what I was thinking. And the look on his face was pure dread.

When the set finished (six games to love), I walked off court without a backward glance. No jokey handshake at the net, no banter, no jovial bowing to the crowd, no crying foul or demanding a rematch. Kit just shrugged, as if to say, *No idea what that was all about.* The onlookers appeared puzzled, except for Mal, who turned away.

We all repaired to dinner, and when Kit tried to put his arm around me, I ducked out and placed myself next to Hope.

Hugo remained silent and strange, though the game had brought him into firm alliance with Alex. He'd encouraged Alex from the start, said he had potential and offered to coach him. Alex was more interested in bats than balls, but as the kid least likely to attract attention from the family, least likely to be singled out for possible talent, least likely to be in on the joke, Hugo's offer pleased him immeasurably. The thought that we'd all misjudged Hugo had occurred to me some time ago, but I watched it take root with the rest of the family. Mum in particular, who'd been too busy to take much notice of Hugo, looked pale with regret and made a special effort to be nice.

He was still liable to get up and walk off without a word, not saying when or if he'd be back, but I was growing accustomed to his weirdness. His best quality was not being bothered about where we went or what we did when we spent time together; he just brought along a sketchbook or something to read and could settle wordlessly for hours.

Sometimes I forgot about him altogether and was surprised when I stood up and saw he was still there.

It was a weird relationship, a bit like mine with Gomez, only with less conversation.

Mum said she was pleased we were getting on better. Kit stayed away. As furious as I was, I missed him trying to seduce me.

The wedding was right on track. Mum and Hope did a trial run with trestle tables and rented folding chairs; the green and blue tablecloths looked glorious in the unmown grass with the sea beyond. Hope wanted to use local ingredients as much as possible, so they spent days visiting farmers' markets. She found a lavender-and-herb farm run by two women who had once worked in finance, a chef who specialized in foraging courses, and a pick-your-own raspberry-and-strawberry farm only a few miles up the road. All recipes were tested on us, so we got to argue about what we liked best.

At dinner Hope always asked Mal how the lines were going, and Mal always gave a sample recital. We were getting to know *Hamlet* pretty well.

"Get thee to a nunnery," Mal said to Hope. *"Why wouldst thou be a breeder of sinners? I am myself indifferent honest, but yet I could accuse me of such things that it were better my mother had not borne me."*

"What things?" Hope frowned. "Is there something I should know?"

Mal threw her a kiss. I glanced at Kit, who was all over Mattie.

Tamsin nearly always slid into dinner late. Despite her broken arm, she spent more time than ever at the yard thanks to her new friend, a boy of all things, who kept a big chestnut gelding called Bilbo and liked to have someone (Tam) admire his jumping.

"Which I do," she explained, "because he's incredible."

The horse or the boy?

Tam was trying to cut a chicken leg with one hand, steadying the meat with her cast. "Which are you more nervous about," she asked Mal. "The wedding or the play?"

Mal frowned at her. "Do you even have to ask? What could be nerve-racking about marrying yon glorious wench?"

"Anyway, it's only a play," Mattie said, and Hope went pale.

"Oh my God, do not *ever* say that about *Hamlet*."

Alex sniggered till Tamsin whacked him.

"Mattie, how is it that you get more ignorant as you get older?" Mal looked genuinely upset. After waiting for a reply that didn't come, he stood up and left the table. It was so unlike his normal behavior that we all felt a bit stunned. Hope went after him, returning a minute later.

Mum exchanged glances with her and sighed. "He's been quite touchy lately, hasn't he?"

"He's genuinely terrified about the play." Kit had his arm around Mattie, who'd stuck her lower lip out but didn't appear to be suffering remorse. "I don't blame him," Kit went on. "And on top of it all, the wedding. Timing could have been better."

"Well, I *am* sorry." Hope glared at Kit, and it was one of the few times I'd ever seen her angry. "God forbid our wedding should get in the way of Mal's career."

"I was just thinking," said Kit quietly, "how hard it must be to enjoy the happiest day of his—"

"Don't bother," Hope snapped, and left the table. Mum got up and began clearing plates.

"Never mind." She placed a hand on Kit's shoulder. "Weddings have a tendency to unsettle people."

"Kit has a tendency to unsettle people," Alex muttered.

I glanced at Hugo. His face was flushed and he vibrated like a steel string. The violence I occasionally glimpsed in him frightened me.

The sky over the sea was clear and pale but in the other direction it had turned an almost greenish black.

I nudged Hugo. "Let's get out of here."

He followed me down to the sea and we sat on the sand. Neither of us spoke, but he seemed to relax a little in my presence. When it started to drizzle, he stood and returned to the house, so I set off along the long path round the back of the lagoons on my own, coming out at the end of the houses where great thickets of hawthorn and scrubby damson provided a windbreak for the fields beyond. The trees made strange configurations, dense but filled with clear passages at ground level, perfect for what we'd imagined as kids were cozy dens for foxes and badgers. When the drizzle turned to rain, I crawled into the center of a thicket, something I hadn't done in a decade. Inside was cramped but dry. It was a good place to sit out a storm.

Watching the rain drip off the hawthorn, I shivered a little in my damp clothes. I'd go home in a few minutes and put on something dry.

The last of the sun struggled out from behind cloud cover and voices drifted over from the next field.

They came closer and I sat silent, secure in my thicket.

Voices. I recognized Mal's. Bloody Hamlet.

"What is the reason that you use me thus? I loved you ever: but it is no matter. Let Hercules himself do what he may, the cat will mew, and dog will have his day . . ."

And then, "Mal," I heard. "Mal . . . Oh God, Mal."

Followed by silence. Not quite silence. Not silence at all.

I couldn't see. I wasn't sure what I was hearing.

What was I hearing?

No, I thought. *Impossible. Not that.*

25

My sister never again looked as beautiful as she did that summer. Throughout her life people continued to remark on her loveliness, but to me she was never the same again. Something fell away.

For what felt like forever, nobody knew. I doubted myself. What was there to know? Perhaps nothing. As the hours passed, my brain second-guessed what it couldn't quite believe.

While I doubted, Hugo drew pictures, Mum sewed, Hope read, Mattie paced. I could see Mattie going through all the options in her head, desperate to be the person Kit loved, not merely the one he sometimes liked. That person was worthless.

Eventually, even the way she walked looked broken.

I didn't know what to do. I barely knew what I knew.

There was always Hugo. At first I avoided him, terrified that he'd confirm what I'd overheard. Hope asked what was wrong and I claimed I was worried about Mattie. She looked at me, sighed, and said nothing.

I searched for meaningful looks: a glance, the brush of a hand. Nothing.

For a day or two the world heaved with fun-house mirrors and distortions, betrayals, uncertainties, false motives, smoke screens. Villains who smiled. Weeping mad girls.

When I picked up my telescope to survey the beach, it swung toward the hawthorn scrub, seemingly of its own accord. Did I see a figure there? Two figures? The telescope burned my fingers. I threw it down on the bed.

I cornered Hugo in the kitchen of Malanhope's. "Are you avoiding me?"

"Yes," he said, which against all odds made me smile.

"What's going on?" I blocked the door so he couldn't escape.

And there it was, the gaze I'd last seen down the

lens of my telescope. Eyes intense, unblinking. He said nothing.

I grabbed his arm and his expression hardened. *Yes,* I thought, *I bloody well know you hate being grabbed. Personally, I hate lies, betrayal, emotional havoc, mayhem — but you don't see me complaining.*

He took a deep breath. "There's something I have to tell you," he said.

I waited, teeth and fists clenched against whatever it was I was going to hear. *Get on with it,* I thought. *Just talk.*

I waited.

"The thing is," he said, and without knowing why, I felt a sudden surge of affection for him, for being so awkward and so purely what he was. The beautiful brother was a desert oasis, a landscape hung upside down in a shimmer of heat. Hugo was the real thing.

"Last summer . . ."

Last summer? I waited.

Hugo began to speak without looking up. "We spent last summer on the coast north of Rome with a director friend of my mother's — Antonio, he was called — and his new wife, Giulia. I think Florence and he had a thing once. The villa was massive, fifteen bedrooms at least. Extended family came and went all the time. There were cooks and housekeepers, dinners for twenty every night. I'd never seen anything like it. Kit made himself at home, took the launch across the bay to swim, played tennis every morning, made friends with everyone, including the cook, convinced Giulia to teach him Italian. They all fell for him, *il bel Americano*. He ended up spending more and more time with Giulia while Antonio was in Rome. It didn't matter that she was twice his age. And when her daughter arrived for the summer, he started hanging around with her, which enraged Giulia. She called Antonio back from Rome and there was an almighty scene. Florence claimed it was all a terrible mistake, but no one believed that. We were ejected that same night, no one even suggesting we wait till morning."

"He was 'hanging around' with the daughter?"

"Yes."

I thought about this. "Well, why not. Good-looking American boy, beautiful Italian girl, it's a pretty obvious recipe for intrigue."

Hugo glanced up. "She was twelve. What I'm trying to tell you is that he's a wrecker." He looked me straight in the eye. "He likes to see what he can get away with. It's a game with him."

I felt a chill. "You make him sound like a psychopath."

Hugo shrugged. "He's an emotional black hole. He sucks the light out of people."

For a moment I felt a kind of vertigo. I wanted to say, *Yes, of course last summer sounds grim, but wasn't this different?* Everything felt so real to me, the whole world Kit Godden created. But when I put it that way, even to myself, I realized exactly how big the fantasy had grown. Smoke and mirrors. A puppet master pulling strings. Us, dancing.

Without exactly knowing why, I leaned in and kissed him and he kissed me back, both of us poleaxed with shock and sadness and desire. I was shaking so hard I could barely stand.

I pulled away. "Hugo?"

It wasn't much of a question and he didn't answer. So I told him what I'd seen. Not seen, exactly. Heard. What I imagined was taking place, what appeared to be taking place.

He looked at me and nodded. A short, unhappy nod. "I didn't know about Mal," he said. There were tears in his eyes.

"Maybe I'm wrong?" I hoped so desperately to be wrong that for an instant I felt certain he'd say, *Of course you are, don't be an idiot,* and it would all be over.

"Oh God," was all he said. He looked sick, distracted.

We stood perfectly still for a long time.

"I'm sorry," he said. "I have to go."

I dragged myself back home. *Look normal*, I thought. *Look normal.*

There was drama still to come. Despite a crushing desire to bring the curtain down on the summer, it wouldn't end. Another week. A wedding and tennis still to come.

Saturday arrived and so did the semifinals. The atmosphere on the beach was unbearable. And yet life went on, while everyone pretended to be fine.

Hope played Mattie and won. They hugged afterward and swore that their daughters would play each other in the tournament someday.

That just left Kit to play Hugo. Hope would play the winner.

I knew that Hugo would never in a million years have put himself in this position willingly. Practically his whole mission in life was to avoid Kit. With a start, I realized I had never seen them exchange a single word. I racked my brain. Not one. Was that even possible? How had I not noticed before?

My family, my poor deluded family, crowded around the boys in separate groups: Hope, Alex, Mum, and me around Hugo; Mattie, Tamsin, Mal, and Dad cheering Kit on. And just then I remembered the cormorant, the bird we'd probably given a heart attack, and Mal's warning at the beginning of the summer not to crowd him to death. I looked at Kit, the golden skin and burnished hair, and all I could see of his beautiful mouth was a beak. The gold-flecked eyes looked small, beady, and red. Instead of defined muscles and long legs, I saw the ragged black wings of the cormorant, the dark soul flapping. I blinked, and the bird disappeared.

Kit threw kisses to the crowd while Hugo stared at his racket, picking the strings. It was traditional to form two cheering squads, but this year we stood on opposite sides of the court, the Kit crew cheerful and chanting, Hugo's gang quiet. Alex looked anxious. Perhaps hanging around with bats had given him the ability to hear portents. I put my hand on his shoulder.

"It's OK," I told him. "We're going to win."

"We fucking well better," said Hope, and I glanced at her, but she was staring straight ahead, her mouth tense.

The players walked to the net and touched rackets briefly. Kit flipped a coin and Hugo called it. Heads. It came up tails. Kit's serve.

I was too tense to breathe.

Kit's game looked good and Hugo didn't even

bother trying to return the first serve. He just stood and watched it go by, and I panicked, worried he would throw the game, refuse to play. Or worse, that he'd be intimidated by his brother, bottle it.

He returned the second serve, but didn't smash it, just went for the volley, a nice soft return to the center of the court, straight and easy to Kit's forehand. He played the rest of the game with a dead hand, stopping the balls, returning them as innocuously as if he were playing with Alex, letting Kit set them up to smash home. He watched them slice past him, didn't run for the wide shots or lunge for the drops. Thirty–love. Forty–love. Game, Kit.

Kit's cheering section went wild, and he threw his arms in the air for a little victory dance. Hugo stood expressionless at the center of the court. It occurred to me that they'd never played each other before. Separate schools and a desire to avoid each other's company — Kit may have been worried at the beginning, but I doubted it. Hugo didn't figure in his plans. He certainly wasn't worried now.

The serve went to Hugo who, with an almost lazy action, tossed the ball into the air, contracting and uncoiling his long frame beneath it in the action I'd admired so much, extending his arm to produce a lightning strike of a serve. With a startled expression, Kit got his racket on it, just, and Hugo sliced a lethal crosscourt for the return. Kit sprinted for a messy thud that just cleared the net, and Hugo fired it back to the opposite corner. You barely saw Hugo move; his volley was clean and sharp as a blade, his face impassive. He seemed to hover on the balls of his feet. The rally went on, Kit sweating, running every ball into the ground, while Hugo barely exerted himself. I'd never seen anything like it. Hugo was smarter, quicker, more accurate. Not a movement wasted, not a foot astray. He played like a Zen master.

The rest of the set was a rout. Like Hope acting in *A Doll's House*, Hugo appeared to do less and less. He didn't run out of breath, he didn't groan and sprint. He just served his deadly serve and ruthlessly, without emotion, won every point.

Game, Hugo.

Game, Hugo.

Game, Hugo.

Kit laughed it off, but as the set went on he grew tired and angry, slapping balls across the net without power, looking more and more frayed. In the final game, Hugo served into a rally that wouldn't end. He returned each parry with a simple shot that even an exhausted, outclassed player could just about hit. So Kit continued to cover the court, panting and sweating and swearing as he tried to smash ball after ball at his brother and watched as each came back, with mechanical precision like balls lobbed out of a practice machine, one after another placed precisely where he could least reach, yet not so far that he could stop running.

It was pure hate, disguised as sport.

At the end of the set, Hugo stood silently in the center of the court while Kit panted, hands on knees, furious. We cheered.

The second set was worse — or better. Hugo humiliated Kit, ran him down, destroyed his balance, ruined his confidence. Kit began missing easy shots, tripping over his own feet. At one point, he threw down his racket in fury. Hugo ignored him, playing on like an automaton. He never met his brother's eyes, not once, until match point, when he took an extra moment, stared directly down the court at Kit, and then, carefully, with excruciating slowness, tossed the ball into the air and kissed it goodbye. There was no chance on earth that his brother would hit it. Kit watched it scream past with a strange expression on his face.

Hope and Alex and I jumped and hugged and ran onto the court and jumped and hugged Hugo, and he rewarded us with a small smile. He was sweating. And then behind his back we watched as Kit made up his mind, decided the only way to regain control of the situation was through détente, approached the net, and stuck out his hand.

Hugo glanced at the hand, looked back up at Kit for a long moment, his pupils black, dilated. Then he turned and walked off court.

It was one of the best moments of my life. Fifty years from now it will still be one of the best moments of my life.

26

Mum and Hope were in our kitchen and, weirdly, Mum was weeping while Hope embraced her.

"It's OK, it's OK," Hope said.

Shouldn't it be the other way around? I tiptoed out before either of them noticed.

Alex waylaid me by the kitchen door looking ashen. "The wedding's off," he said, obviously waiting for me to say, "Oh my God! Why?" Which I didn't.

"I know" was all I said, and Alex glared at me.

"No you don't," he said. "Nobody knew till just right now."

I nodded at him and as I walked away I heard him on the phone, knowing it would be Dad, caught on his way to the post office. I returned to the kitchen and this time Hope saw me, and with a tired look said, "You'd better sit down."

I sat down, and she told me that Mal had come to her and said he couldn't go through with it, which was fair enough, only there was more. He was in love with someone else.

Hope brushed the hair back from her face. She looked at me and frowned.

"You knew?" she said.

I didn't answer.

"Does Mattie know?" I'd been thinking about Mattie, had already rationalized that she was well out of it, but of course she wouldn't be feeling well out of it at all. Mattie and most of the rest of the human race would see the events pure and simply as betrayal. I doubted whether she'd even manage to spare much of a thought for Hope. But in this I was wrong.

Mattie entered the kitchen at that moment and walked straight up to Hope, embraced her, and said, "He's a shit, Hope. And Mal's deluded. Like I was." Then she drew back and looked gravely at Hope and said, "I feel quite sorry for him, actually."

Well, what do you know, that's when I started to cry, because it was literally the first time that I realized how much I'd underestimated my sister. Theirs was the most graceful exchange of the whole miserable event, and a blind person could see that Hope was moved by it. Mum didn't embrace Mattie. But she watched with a kind of furious pride.

Hope told us that Mal had gone to London to stay with a friend. He'd left Gomez behind, for now.

"I asked him to go," she told us. I wondered how she stood it, keeping hold of Gomez, like Mal's unwanted child.

A phone call was placed that evening to Florence, and she sent a car to fetch the boys. It arrived so quickly that I wondered if she kept one on standby for just such emergencies. I heard later how she'd written a brief note to Hope saying she was terribly sorry but wouldn't make it to the wedding. I guess no one bothered to ask, "What wedding?"

And here's something else. None of the tears and unhappiness of people I loved meant as much to me as you might think, because despite everything, I kept thinking about Hugo, a slim shaft of light in the darkness.

27

Back in my tower I saw Hope walking down to the water. I didn't have a lot of qualms about spying—but watching her cry felt wrong and I looked away.

I loved Hope, and I loved Mal, and I hoped Mal knew what he was doing, though it seemed pretty clear that he didn't.

When the car did arrive, Hugo made himself scarce and Mum came through like a hero, saying he didn't have to go right away and could stay with us till the dust settled. We didn't see Kit go.

Tamsin was up at the barn, so it was suppertime before she heard the news. It barely seemed to register at first, which convinced me once and for all that for her the real world — the world without horses — was just some sort of shadowland.

"Why would he do that?" she asked eventually, and no one quite knew which "he" she was talking about, though it didn't really matter. Either way, there was no answer.

Over the days that followed, Hugo and I spent most of our time together. Alex often appeared, uncharacteristically silent, grabbing Hugo's arm and refusing to let go. Hugo didn't seem to mind being grabbed by Alex.

It took Hope two days to contact everyone on the guest list, cancel the caterers, and shut up the house, and then she took Gomez and left, having talked just to Mum and Dad, who reported that she was sorry not to say goodbye personally to the rest of us but she sent her love. She didn't take the wedding outfit. I asked Mum what she was going to do with it and she looked at me in surprise. I guess she hadn't had time to think about it.

The house vibrated with shock, and everyone tiptoed around as if someone had died. Mum seemed even worse hit than Hope and burst into tears every so often over not very much. As for Mattie, she rose from the ashes of her glorious love affair like a phoenix.

"He made me much more unhappy than happy," she said. "It was like being possessed."

I knew what she meant.

We didn't talk about it openly because of Hugo; we didn't want to cause him pain. Family opinion had pivoted and everyone felt thoroughly guilty, having been so wrong about both brothers for so long.

It was Hugo who broached the subject the next night at dinner.

"I'm sorry," he announced in an almost formal manner. "I'm sorry for my brother's behavior. And I'm sorry still to be here to remind you of it. We've ruined everything. Your summer." He paused. "And Hope's life."

Mum put her arms around Hugo and hugged him like a child. "It's not your fault," she said, adding sternly, "Hope's life isn't ruined—imagine marrying an actor! It was a lucky escape."

Hugo suffered the embrace for a minute, then pulled away. "I knew it would go horribly wrong because when Kit's around it always does. But I couldn't stop it." His face seemed to sag. "I wanted to, I thought it was only Mattie he would hurt . . ." He looked at Mattie. "I don't mean only. It mattered so much. I tried." The look he gave her touched me deeply; it was full of sorrow.

"You did," Mattie said, and shrugged. "It's OK,

Hugo. I appreciate that you tried. But I'm OK. And what's done is done."

And I thought: *the Scottish play. That makes a nice change.*

Hugo looked exhausted.

"Anyway," Tam said. "Nobody could have predicted."

This could not have been less true. Hugo predicted. He'd warned me numerous times. And even if he hadn't, I should have known, and might have too if I hadn't been so flattered by the attention. Wanted it so much to be real.

Mum suggested that whoever felt like it should go for a walk. Mattie got up and they went off together. In all this mess, she didn't get as much attention as she should have; it wasn't just Hope's heart dragged through the mud. But she bore it with dignity and we all thought the same thing at the same time, that it was time to stop treating her like a child.

None of them consoled me, of course. No one knew. Except for Hugo, whose consolation took the form of friendship. And against all odds I was consoled.

Malcolm was gone. It was the last any of us saw of him for a long time. He went on to do *Hamlet* but the reviews were not kind.

We didn't go.

28

Hugo refused to go back to LA. His mother didn't want him, though you'd never guess from her weeping protests.

"I don't mind if you stay here," Mum said. Come and be part of a family was what she meant.

So he joined us, kind of. You couldn't rag him or ask how he felt, and instead of bickering and taking sides in every argument like the rest of us, he'd just back off. But he was the truest person I ever met and any triumph I felt at recognizing Kit's treachery was eclipsed by missing Hugo's value from the start.

Mal's affair with Kit didn't last. He regained custody of Gomez but didn't contact any of us. He was probably too ashamed.

The following summer Hope had the house on the beach to herself. She had a new friend, called Tomas, who visited in August. He was not an actor and we decided to like him for at least as long as Hope did. Hugo stayed in our house. Mattie spent most of her time studying. Tamsin leased Duke again. Alex and Dad registered three species of bat they'd never seen before on the beach.

Mum dyed Hope's wedding dress indigo, altered the shoulders, and wore it herself to the opera.

And I did the usual not very much. I drew pictures, went swimming, hung around with my family. Hugo and I talked, sailed boats, drew pictures. We talked about art school and what we might do someday. I felt less urgency to experience all that life had to offer, all emotions, all at once. My future was still uncertain. What would I do? How would I know what to choose?

When the impulse arose, I surveyed the beach through my telescope and sometimes did sketches of what I saw. If the day happened to be clear, I saw seals and sailboats and cargo ships and electrical storms with forked lightning and vertical dark streaks of rain in the distance. I saw a cormorant standing black and ragged against the sky. Occasionally, when my eyes were closed, I glimpsed slivers of my future. Sometimes silver, sometimes dark.

Time would tell.

When I look back on that summer, it's always with a sense of having lost something fragile and fleeting, something I can't quite name. We still go to the beach and still have good times, but it's never quite the same.

After a few years we lost track of Kit Godden. Last I heard he was back living in LA. Hugo says he never wants to see him again. He says, "Who cares what happens to that bastard?"

Well, I don't.

I don't.

Obviously, I don't.

But I do still think of that face and those hands and a voice telling me that I'm something else.

And more and more I think that maybe he was right.